"I really am sorry, Lucy," Nick said softly.

When Lucy finally stopped crying, she asked, "May I use your handkerchief, please?"

"You can use my scarf. I don't mind."

The offer to use Nick's scarf to dry her eyes and blow her nose was so ridiculous and sweet it caused Lucy to chuckle. "*Neh*, that's okay," she said, removing her mittens to dab her tears.

"I'm sorry I treated you that way. I didn't mean to. I care about you, and I wouldn't want anything to happen to you. I especially wouldn't want to play a role in hurting you."

Lucy was overwhelmed. No man had ever said anything like that to her before, even in friendship. "It's not your fault," she said. "And I do appreciate that you care. But I'm not as fragile as you think I am."

"Fragile? You? I don't think you're fragile at all," Nick scoffed. "I think you're one of the most resilient women I've ever known."

Lucy was overwhelmed again. If this kept up, she was going to fall hard for Nick Burkholder. Maybe she already had…

Carrie Lighte lives in Massachusetts next door to a Mennonite farming family, and she frequently spots deer, foxes, fisher cats, coyotes and turkeys in her backyard. Having enjoyed traveling to several Amish communities in the eastern United States, she looks forward to visiting settlements in the western states and in Canada. When she's not reading, writing or researching, Carrie likes to hike, kayak, bake and play word games.

Books by Carrie Lighte

Love Inspired

Amish Country Courtships

Amish Triplets for Christmas
Anna's Forgotten Fiancé
An Amish Holiday Wedding
Minding the Amish Baby
Her New Amish Family
Her Amish Holiday Suitor

Visit the Author Profile page at Harlequin.com.

Her Amish Holiday Suitor

Carrie Lighte

LOVE INSPIRED BOOKS

Recycling programs
for this product may
not exist in your area.

ISBN-13: 978-1-335-47944-0

Her Amish Holiday Suitor

Copyright © 2019 by Carrie Lighte

www.Harlequin.com

Printed in U.S.A.

For the Lord seeth not as man seeth;
for man looketh on the outward appearance,
but the Lord looketh on the heart.
—*1 Samuel* 16:7

For the readers who have followed
my Amish Country Courtships series,
with much gratitude for your interest
and best wishes for your lives.

Chapter One

"You did *what*?" Nick Burkholder asked as he guided his horse along the dark, winding country roads of Willow Creek, Pennsylvania. It was the Sunday after Thanksgiving, and he and his brother were on their way to a singing at Frederick Stutzman's house. Their plan was to make a brief appearance and then leave to hang out with Nick's Amish friends from Elmsville at an eatery in Highland Springs.

"On Friday night I, uh, sort of started a fire in Jenny Nelson's cabin," seventeen-year-old Kevin repeated, referring to the vacation house of an *Englisch* acquaintance.

The redheaded brothers were known for kidding around, so Nick assumed Kevin was joking. "Oh, I get it. You mean you started a fire in their fireplace. You sounded so serious you had me going for a minute there. *Voll schpass.*"

"I wish it were very funny," Kevin replied, using the *Englisch* term for *voll schpass*. It seemed to Nick his brother had picked up more *Englisch* phrases and habits during the first six months of his *rumspringa* than Nick had learned during the entirety of his own five-year running around period.

Kevin's voice was somber as he continued. "I mean, *jah*, initially I was trying to start a fire in the fireplace, but one of the newspaper logs I rolled must have—"

"Kevin!" Nick cut him off. "You should know better than to use newspaper logs after all the warnings *Daed*'s given you!"

"I just thought—"

"*Neh*, that's just the problem. You didn't *think* at all," Nick retorted, ironically using the same words his father often used when lecturing *him*. He brought the buggy to a standstill at the side of the road and turned to face Kevin. "Please tell me no one was injured."

"*Neh*. But there was a little superficial damage to the walls and ceiling."

Kevin proceeded to tell Nick he must have been distracted by the other guests summoning him into the kitchen to eat, because he forgot to close the protective mesh screen on the fireplace. He reckoned when someone opened the door to the cabin it created a back draft, and ash from the dry newspaper logs was swept through the air, because the next thing anyone knew, a pair of window curtains caught fire. The flames quickly leaped to a dried floral wreath hanging on the wall nearby, and before Jenny could retrieve the extinguisher, the wood paneling and ceiling had been burned, too.

Nick's mind was reeling, and he could hardly focus on the additional details Kevin provided about the mishap. If only Nick had attended the party with him, the fire probably wouldn't have happened. But Nick's parents had requested Nick stay behind and help take inventory at the hardware store his father owned.

"You just went out on Wednesday night. You're too old to be gallivanting around at every opportunity," his mother had said in a tone that indicated she meant business. "Your *daed* needs your help organizing and stocking up on specialty products the *Englisch* buy for *Grischtdaag*. Friday evening is the only opportunity he has."

Nick couldn't refuse. At twenty-one, he'd stretched out his *rumspringa* longer than almost anyone in his church district, which was a point of contention between his parents and him. They strongly implied if he didn't decide to join the church soon, he'd have to move out on his own. While he wouldn't be shunned, it would be disgracing for the entire family if he lived apart from them but stayed in the Amish community without being baptized into the church.

The choice should have been an easy one, and deep down, Nick had already made up his mind. He loved God, he loved being Amish and he loved his community. By now he knew that although some aspects of *Englisch* life were appealing, he had no desire to "go *Englisch*" for good. But he was also keenly aware that as long as he didn't join the church, he wouldn't be permitted to marry an Amish woman. And although he had courted most of the eligible young women in Willow Creek, as well as several from the Elmsville district, he hadn't met anyone he considered compatible enough to marry. Apparently, the same wasn't true for how the women felt about him; when he inevitably broke up with them, the women often expressed deep disappointment. Worse, they cried as if there were no tomorrow, no matter how gentle or diplomatic he tried to be about ending their courtship.

To Nick it seemed the women he courted didn't really care whether they were compatible with him. It was as if they were more interested in being married than being in a marriage *relationship*. Granted, there was no mandate requiring Nick to get married once he joined the church, but it was generally expected. Once he was baptized, the pressure—especially from his mother—would really kick in. So, by prolonging his *rumspringa*, Nick was securing his bachelorhood just a little longer. Meanwhile, someone new might move to town. After all, a spouse was a gift from the Lord, and who could say when and how the Lord might give him that gift?

Kevin spoke again, jarring Nick from his thoughts. "Jenny said if I pay for the repairs, she'll hire a contractor and then she won't have to tell her folks about the fire. So, can you lend me the money? Since we're passing Jenny's house on the way to Highland Springs, I sort of promised her I'd let her know tonight."

"Are you *narrish*?" Nick asked, calling his brother *crazy*. "I cleaned out my savings to purchase Penny last spring."

Penny, named for the color of his coat, was the horse Nick bought from an Amish man who had acquired the animal at a harness racing track. It wasn't unusual for the Amish to purchase American standardbred horses, which were most commonly used for buggy pulling, and Penny was a particularly fine gelding. Only four years old, he was exceptionally fast and strong, although not quite up to competition speed. As such, he cost more than the four-thousand-dollar limit most of Willow Creek's Amish spent on a horse, but Nick had saved for years. When he took Penny out for a test run, he immediately knew the swift, powerful, high-spirited animal was exactly what he wanted.

The cost was another point of contention between him and his parents, who thought it was foolish to splurge when an older, less expensive standardbred would have served his transportation needs adequately for years to come. His parents thought the purchase was prideful, but Nick wasn't seeking admiration; it was the speed and agility the horse provided that drew Nick to him. True, Penny could only safely run so fast when he was hitched to the buggy, but Nick had made adjustments to streamline his buggy, too. Those adjustments had cost him every last cent he had, and he reiterated that he was in no position to help his brother financially.

"Oh." In the dim light, Nick saw Kevin's features droop as he lifted his hat and swiped at his forehead. "I guess I'm going to have to tell *Daed* then."

"That's not a *gut* idea. You know how concerned he's been about finances ever since Harper's Hardware opened across town. And you know how worried *Mamm* is about his blood pressure and stress levels."

Kevin shrugged. "I don't know what else to do."

Nick rubbed his forehead. He didn't know what else to do, either, but telling their father was the last thing he could allow. Not only was he concerned about adding to his parents' burdens, but somehow Nick knew he'd get blamed for introducing Kevin to a group of "wild *Englischers*"—even if they were all very respectable Christians and the fire was solely Kevin's fault. Undoubtedly, his father would be so angry about Kevin's carelessness that he'd finally put his foot down about

Nick's *rumspringa* coming to an end, too. Nick couldn't let that happen.

"Give me a minute. I'll think of something," he said.

Twenty-year-old Lucy Knepp dawdled in the kitchen, drying the last pot. Usually the Amish didn't eat a large supper on the Sabbath, but there were so many leftovers from Thanksgiving they had dirtied half a dozen pans reheating the food. Lucy's stepsisters, Mildred and Katura, stepped into the kitchen just as she was hanging up the dishcloth.

"There you are." Mildred sounded triumphant, as if it were unusual to find Lucy cleaning up after supper.

Actually, Lucy did the majority of the housework, cooking and baking for her family. Born eight weeks prematurely, she had suffered respiratory problems since birth, which prevented her from helping with yard work, gardening and cleaning the stable, so she tried to make up for it by taking on more chores inside their home.

"You must *kumme* with us to Frederick's *haus* for the singing. We're also going to plan our *Grischtdaag* caroling rehearsal schedule," Katura announced.

Lucy didn't want to go with them. For one thing, Frederick had passed several notes to her at previous singings, a sure sign he was preparing to ask to be her suitor. Even though she'd tactfully but distinctly ignored his pursuit, his interest hadn't waned. Frederick was a nice enough young man, but Lucy had no interest in being courted by him. She had no interest in being courted by *any* of the single men in Willow Creek, for that matter. By and large they seemed too rambunctious and unreliable for her to imagine ever becoming a wife to one of them.

Likewise, Lucy had long ago accepted that she wasn't the kind of vibrant, vivacious woman most Willow Creek boys would want to court. With the exception of Frederick, who probably liked her because she was the only eligible woman who was shorter than he was—not to mention that his rather aggressive mother was especially fond of Lucy. Lucy had overheard enough comments to understand the bachelors in Willow Creek considered her personality to be dull. She realized her physical appearance didn't appeal to the men her age, either. She had plain brown eyes and ordinary brown hair. Her only distinctive features were her glasses—which earned her the nickname "Bug Eyes" in school—and her petite size, which made it even easier for young men to overlook her.

"You go ahead without me," Lucy suggested to her stepsisters. "I'll stay and help Betty clean up." Lucy had never known her own mother, who had died in childbirth, but in the five years since Betty had become her stepmother, Lucy still couldn't bring herself to call Betty *"Mamm,"* and she was glad when Betty didn't insist.

"But everything is cleaned and put away already. And you know *Mamm* won't let us go unless you *kumme,* too."

She was right. Even though Mildred was eighteen and Katura was the same age as Lucy, Betty was likely to prohibit her daughters from going out unless Lucy went with them. Sunday evening singings were intended to be a time of fellowship and fun for young people, but Lucy noticed the majority of Willow Creek's singles only went to the singings so they'd have an excuse to get out of their houses. They'd make a brief showing at the host house, where they participated in a few songs, and then they'd pair up to take off for parties or wherever it was they went.

Half the time Lucy brought a book so she could slip away to a corner to read. She frequently returned home without either Mildred or Katura, who would sneak off before she realized they had ditched her. By that time, her father and Betty were usually asleep, and the next day Lucy never mentioned where her sisters had gone.

"But I was planning to work on an embroidery project," Lucy objected.

"Work isn't permitted on the Sabbath," Katura scolded, as if Lucy weren't always meticulous about following the rules of her district's *Ordnung*.

With all the patience she could muster, Lucy explained, "This isn't something I'm going to consign at Schrock's Shop. It's the tablecloth-and-napkin set for the charity auction at the Piney Hill Christmas festival."

Since embroidering was quiet, sedentary work and the project wasn't for her own financial profit, Lucy felt she could work on the project on the Sabbath in good conscience. Moreover, she *needed* to work on the project that evening.

Her deadline for completing it was December 21, when the linens would be displayed with other items in a silent auction to benefit the *Englisch* soup kitchen where she volunteered on Wednesday nights. Interested buyers would have two days to bid on the goods and Lucy and her family planned to attend the festival the evening of the twenty-third, when the highest bid was announced. Last year she'd been sick with pneumonia and wasn't able to participate in any fundraising events for the soup kitchen. This year the organization was so strapped it couldn't even afford to repair their commercial oven, and they were counting on Lucy's contribution to raise at least half the funds they needed.

"Can't you do that tomorrow? You're home all day."

Mildred's ignorance was insulting; Lucy may have been home all day, but when she wasn't keeping house her time was spent working on items she consigned at Schrock's Shop so she could contribute to their family's living expenses. As it was, Lucy could barely manage to fill the customers' specialty orders for Christmas. She'd have to keep all unnecessary distractions to a minimum if she was going to complete the auction project on time, too. Unfortunately, she realized her stepsisters would keep wheedling until she gave in, and that in itself would be a distraction.

"Okay," she agreed. "But you have to take care of unhitching the buggy and stabling the horse when we get home." The weather was turning cold and she couldn't afford to get sick.

"Sure. We wouldn't want you exerting yourself," Mildred said, and Lucy didn't know if she was being sarcastic or sincere.

"*Mamm!* We're leaving now," Katura called after the trio bundled into their winter cloaks and donned their gloves. Lucy never understood why Betty didn't tell her daughters it wasn't polite to shout in the house. "We'll be home before midnight."

Midnight? Lucy didn't even want to stay past nine, but when she opened her mouth to protest, she quickly closed it again. Arguing would cost her more time. Instead, she said, "I'll be right back."

She darted upstairs and grabbed her embroidery materials and carefully placed them in a canvas bag. She figured by midnight she could probably finish embroidering at least one of the napkins—provided she could find a secluded place where no one would interrupt her.

After a few minutes of silence, Nick said, "I'll talk to Jenny about the damage. Maybe there's a way I can make the repairs myself." Having worked with his uncle's carpentry crew for a year when his uncle was ill, Nick was a better craftsman than Kevin.

"But when?" Kevin questioned. "It's not a one-day job. You know we won't get any Saturdays off until after *Grischtdaag*." He went on to explain that Jenny's family was planning a Christmas Eve reunion in the cabin with her ailing grandfather, who was traveling all the way from Spokane, Washington, to celebrate the holiday with them.

"I'll have to work on it in the evenings then, won't I?" Nick didn't try to temper his irritation at his brother.

Kevin snorted. "The store is open late on weeknights until *Grischtdaag*, too. There's no way *Mamm* and *Daed* will let you get out of helping."

"Actually, there is. *You're* going to insist you can cover for me at the store."

Kevin's jaw dropped. "I already told them I want to go caroling this year. If I have to stay late at the store, I'll miss the rehearsals during the week."

"Well, unless the money drops from the sky or you suddenly develop expert carpentry skills, you'll have to tell them you changed your mind," Nick advised, annoyed that Kevin still didn't comprehend the sacrifice he was making for him. "Besides, you're not interested in caroling. You just want to get out of working at night during the week."

Kevin didn't deny it. "So what excuse are you going to give *Mamm* and *Daed* for going out on weeknights?" he asked.

"Maybe I'll say *I'm* joining the carolers." Even as he suggested the idea, Nick knew it wasn't plausible. For as many singings as he'd been to, he hardly ever sang. He couldn't carry a tune and his parents knew it, but because singings were chaperoned, they didn't discourage him from attending. "Or maybe I'll tell them I'm courting someone."

"Who? You've already courted all the *meed* in Willow Creek," Kevin countered.

Courtships among the Amish were usually private matters and Nick definitely hadn't told Kevin about his romantic relationships. "How would you know?"

"Word gets around. Everyone says you're a real heartbreaker," Kevin replied flippantly. "You'd practically have to leave Lancaster County to find someone you haven't already courted."

Nick was suddenly inspired. "Hey, maybe someone has a cousin visiting Willow Creek for the Thanksgiving holiday. Let's stop at Frederick's *haus* and check it out. Then we can go talk to Jenny about the repairs."

But when they entered Frederick's home and Nick scanned the room, his hope flagged. The only out-of-towner present was Frederick's cousin, Mark. The usual young women from Willow Creek and the Elmsville district were encircling him, batting their lashes and fiddling with their *kapp* strings. Katura and Mildred Peachy, Lucy Knepp's stepsisters, appeared downright enraptured, and it occurred to Nick he hadn't ever courted either of them. But asking to walk out with Katura or Mildred was a risk he couldn't take. He'd heard how outspoken the sisters had been about wanting to get married at the slightest hint of interest from young men who weren't even their suitors yet. That was exactly the kind of pressure Nick wanted to prevent.

He nudged Kevin, muttering "Let's get out of here," but just then Frederick's mother noticed them and insisted they take off their coats and have some hot chocolate. They couldn't refuse since she was the hosting chaperone, so they gave her their coats and shuffled into the kitchen. After eating popcorn and downing their mugs of cocoa, Nick meandered to the back room to grab their jackets so they could head to Jenny's house.

He had to dig through a heap of coats and cloaks piled on the bed before he found theirs. He was about to exit the room when he caught a small movement out of the corner of his eye. It was Lucy Knepp sitting in a circle of faint lamplight, her head bowed. Was she praying? No, she was sewing.

That was typical. Ever since they were in school Lucy had distanced herself from the other scholars. At recess she always stayed inside and cleaned the whiteboards. It was generally accepted she was the teacher's pet, and the boys believed she spied on them from the window and tattled about their wrongdoings to the teacher. More than once Nick received a scolding for antics on the playground the teacher couldn't have known about unless Lucy had told her.

She probably had matured by now, but she was still

one of the most boring women he'd ever met—either that, or she was a snob, because she made no attempt at even the most casual of conversations. But she was respected by virtually all the parents in Willow Creek, who admired her good manners and quiet thoughtfulness, as well as her dedication to serving the less fortunate *Englischers* in their community.

Because Lucy didn't look up from her fabric, Nick decided he'd pussyfoot it out of the room without greeting her, but suddenly an idea struck him. *She* could be his pretend girlfriend! The plan unfolded almost instantly in his mind's eye: Kevin could "accidentally" let it slip in front of their parents Nick was courting Lucy. Once they heard that, they'd let him go out whenever he wanted, no questions asked.

But how would he convince Lucy he wanted to be her suitor? They were as different as salt and pepper. She'd never believe he genuinely wanted to court her, and even if she did believe it, there was no way she'd accept his offer. The only time they'd really spoken to each other had been when Nick was courting her cousin Bridget. But after Bridget broke up with him three years ago, Lucy hardly looked in his direction. *I'll have to tell her the truth*, Nick concluded. Or some version of the truth. He'd have to present his situation in a way that appealed to her sense of charity and compassion.

"Eh-hem." When Nick cleared his throat, Lucy glanced up and the lenses in her glasses reflected the weak lamplight. How could she see to sew? "Hi, Lucy."

"Hello, Nick," she replied, and adjusted her glasses on her nose. She gestured to the coats he was tightly gripping. "Do you want me to turn the lamp up or did you find what you came in here to get?"

"*Jah*," he replied, stalling.

"*Jah* you want me to turn the lamp up or *jah* you found what you needed?" she asked. Was she smirking or smiling at him?

"I've got my coat, *jah*," he said, glad the light was low so she couldn't watch his face turn as red as his hair. Why was he so nervous? He'd proposed courtship over a dozen times before and he'd never felt like this. "I actually, er, came looking for you."

"For me?" She cocked her head.

"*Jah*. There's a favor I'd like to ask."

Lucy didn't know what to make of Nick's behavior, but there was definitely something fishy about it. It reminded her of his tomfoolery when they'd attended school together. As he shifted from foot to foot she sensed he was there to deliver a joke, and she wanted him to get it over with so she could return to her embroidery. The lighting was terrible and she'd already had to undo her stitching several times, but she didn't want to turn the lamp up, lest she be discovered by dauntless Frederick or his pushy mother, Mary.

"Okay, what's the favor?"

"It's going to sound…it's going to sound *lecherich*. But I wondered if you'd consider allowing me to court you. I mean, I don't really want to court you, I just don't know who else to ask. You see—"

"You're right, that does sound *lecherich*," she interrupted, appalled he'd point out how ridiculous it was for him to consider courting her and then have the gall to admit he was only asking her because he'd run out of other prospects. "And I don't want to be courted by you, either."

She dipped her head and squinted at her stitching, hoping he'd scram. Did he think she'd be so enamored of him she'd gleefully accept his half-hearted offer, the way so many other women in Willow Creek had? They all knew he'd never be serious about sustaining a romantic relationship, but that didn't stop them from saying yes.

Even Lucy's favorite cousin, Bridget, had fallen for him—and then he'd broken her heart by striking up a relationship with someone else before his courtship with Bridget was over. Lucy was smarter than that. She didn't care how charismatic or impishly handsome anyone considered him to be, she didn't need the affections of Nick Burkholder to make her feel special.

"Lucy, please listen," he pleaded.

She glared in his direction and snapped, "What?"

Nick delved into a story about his *Englisch* friends, the Nelson family, whose vacation cabin was damaged by a small fire while Mr. and Mrs. Nelson were away for the Thanksgiving holiday. The family was anticipating celebrating Christmas together there one last time with their dying grandfather, but the parents didn't know the interior was a wreck. Nick's friend didn't want to add to their distress by telling them about the damage since they were already distraught about the grandfather's health. The goal was to complete the repairs before Mrs. Nelson began decorating the cabin for their party.

"I'm pretty confident I can get it all spruced up in time for their celebration, but I need a *gut* excuse to go out in the evenings to work on it. That's where a courtship with you figures in."

Lucy was skeptical. The whole story was probably a fabrication, and she wouldn't be surprised if Nick's friends were listening at the door to hear if she'd fall for it. "Why don't you just tell your *eldre* the real reason you need to go out? They're warmhearted people. They'd want you to help."

Nick rambled, "Like I said, Mr. and Mrs. Nelson don't even know about the fire, so I've got to keep it a secret that I'm renovating the walls. And, I, uh, I probably shouldn't be telling you this but my *daed*'s health has suffered and he's been under quite a bit of financial strain ever since Harper's Hardware came to town. In order to compete with them, we have to keep our store open late until *Grischtdaag*. Even though my brother absolutely can handle the customers without me, since the Nelsons are *Englischers*, well, my *daed* would probably say our family's business takes top priority." Nick wiped his palms against his trousers, casting his gaze toward the floor as he admitted, "If I were courting someone, that would be a different story, because my *eldre* are sort of eager to see me…to see me settle down, as you might imagine."

Lucy *could* imagine. Two Sundays ago after church, Mildred had babbled about how she'd overheard Nick's mother complaining to Doris Plank that she was worried Nick would never join the church and get married. Hearing that, Katura had sulked all the way home because Nick had never asked to be *her* suitor.

"Please, Lucy?" Nick entreated, and she suddenly understood why her peers said yes to walking out with him. There was something irresistible about his earnest manner, his big blue eyes, and the way his nose and cheeks were speckled with freckles. "My friend's *groossdaadi* might not live long enough to return to

Willow Creek, but if he does, he'll be devastated to find his boyhood cabin in tatters."

Lucy's resolve was beginning to waver. She wanted the Nelsons and their grandfather to have a merry Christmas, especially if it was going to be their last celebration together.

"Please?" he repeated.

At that moment Frederick walked in. "Aha, I found you! There's something I want to ask you, Lucy."

Clearly Lucy wasn't going to get anything done tonight. She stashed her embroidery hoop in the canvas tote at her side. Allowing Nick's question to hang in the air unanswered, she turned her attention to Frederick. "Go ahead and ask."

"It's, uh, it's sort of private. So, um, I can wait until you and Nick are done talking."

Lucy had a feeling she knew what Frederick was going to ask and she wished he'd leave her alone. She wished *everyone* would leave her alone and stop forcing their social agendas on her. Then it occurred to her if Frederick thought she was walking out with Nick, he wouldn't ask her to walk out with *him*. Furthermore, if her stepsisters and stepmother thought she was walking out with someone, they wouldn't pester her to join their pre-Christmas social events or the caroling rehearsals, either. She'd finally have time to finish her project.

She stood up and rummaged through the coats, simultaneously saying, "Well, Nick and I were about to head out together, so you might as well ask me now. Nick, would you mind giving Frederick and me a quick moment alone to chat?"

A look of utter surprise crossed Nick's face before

it brightened with elation. "Sure," he said. "I'll wait for you in my buggy."

"Denki," she replied in a syrupy voice, tilting her chin upward for added effect. After Nick left, she asked Frederick, "What is it you want to ask me?"

He stammered, "Oh, er, I was wondering if you'll be caroling this year? In a few minutes we're going to start the meeting to plan our rehearsal schedule and I thought you'd want to make suggestions about meeting times since I know you volunteer during the week."

"Denki for the heads-up, Frederick. But as much as I might enjoy caroling, I have…I have other social engagements that will be taking up my time."

Frederick looked forlorn, but he nodded and said he understood. She almost felt sorry for him, but then his mother entered the room, turned up the lamp and uttered, "Oh *gut,* I see Frederick tracked you down, Lucy! We didn't know where you'd escaped to. I set a mug of cocoa for each of you near the love seat."

A mix of embarrassment and empathy washed over Lucy as she noticed Frederick cringing. She nearly told him she'd stay after all, but Frederick said, "Lucy's going home now. Nick Burkholder is taking her."

"Nick Burkholder?" Frederick's mother was obviously incredulous. There'd be no stopping the rumors from spreading now.

Lucy excused herself quickly, saying, *"Jah,* and he's waiting for me in his buggy, so I'd better get going. *Denki* for your hospitality, Mary. *Gut nacht,* Frederick."

Speechless, Frederick lifted his hand in a wave. He looked stunned, but not nearly as stunned as Mildred and Katura appeared when Lucy bade them goodbye and informed them Nick was giving her a ride home.

"Why? Are you sick?" Mildred asked. "Because if you are, you can take the buggy and Katura and I can get a ride home from someone else. Maybe Frederick's cousin will take us."

"*Neh*, I'm not sick. It's just… Nick and I are…" Lucy allowed the innuendo to hang in the air before concluding, "I'll—I'll see you at home."

Leaving them with their mouths hanging open, Lucy couldn't help but feel a bit smug—not because they were surprised Nick was taking her home, but because for once they really would have to unhitch the buggy and stable the horse by themselves.

Chapter Two

❧

Nick could have jumped for joy when Lucy accepted his offer of courtship. Or of pretend courtship. Before exiting Frederick's house, he signaled Kevin to follow him to the porch.

"Listen, I found someone I can pretend I'm walking out with. The important thing is you can't tell anyone—and I mean *anyone*—that it's not an authentic courtship. If word gets out this is a farce, it will only be a matter of minutes until *Mamm* and *Daed* find out about the fire and then we'll both be in trouble. You got it?" Nick tapped his finger against Kevin's chest, emphasizing his point.

"I got it," he promised, before slyly remarking, "So who's the fortunate *maedel*? I didn't see anyone inside you haven't already courted. Are you going to give one of them a second chance?"

Nick didn't appreciate Kevin's attitude toward young women, and his response was immediate and gruff. "I've already told you it's no one's business what *meed* I've courted in the past. Besides, what makes you think they'd give *me* a second chance?"

"I've always heard you're a charmer, that's all. It was intended as a compliment."

Hearing the admiration in his brother's voice, Nick set him straight. "Courting a lot of *meed* isn't necessarily a *gut* thing, Kevin. Neither is superficial charm. It's the quality, not the quantity of relationships, that's important. Courtship is intended to be an opportunity to discover if you and a *maedel* are compatible for marriage, but regardless of how long your relationships last, you'd better treat any woman you court with respect."

"You sound just like *Daed*, you know that?"

"That's because *Daed*'s right." Nick warned, "You've got your whole *rumspringa* in front of you. Your running around period is a time for you to make decisions on your own. There's a lot of freedom in that, but there's a lot of responsibility, too. I'll help you clean up the mess you've made this time, but if you make another one, you're going to have to take care of it yourself, understand?"

"*Jah, jah*, I got it already. So you still haven't told me who you're going to pretend you're courting."

Nick lowered his voice. "Lucy Knepp."

"Lucy Knepp?" Kevin chortled. "No one will ever believe you're interested in her. She's such a wallflower! Haven't you noticed how pale she is? I don't think she ever goes outside in daytime except to attend church. She's such a goody-goody."

"Exactly. Which is why *Mamm* and *Daed* won't object if they think I'm going out with her during the week," Nick reasoned. "So here's what's going to happen now. While I'm bringing Lucy to her *haus*, you're going to walk to ours. *Mamm* and *Daed* will still be awake and when they ask where I am, you can let it slip

I'm taking Lucy home. Plant the seed in their minds, okay?"

"But what about going to Highland Springs like we planned?"

Nick shrugged. "I already told Lucy I'd take her home. If you still want to go to Highland Springs, go ahead and go. Just make sure you ask whoever gives you a ride to swing by Jenny's *haus* first so you can tell her you can't afford the cost of repairs to the cabin." Before turning to leave, he tossed Kevin's jacket at him and added, "Her *eldre* probably will just contact *Daed* instead of getting the police involved."

That got Kevin's attention. "Wait! I'll do it. I'll walk home now."

"Gut," Nick said. "And remember, you can't let on to anyone—not even Lucy—that you know this is a sham."

"Is it a sham?" Kevin jibed as he shoved his arm through his coat sleeve. "Or could it be this is the opportunity you've been waiting for your entire *rumspringa*? To court Lucy Knepp?"

Nick elbowed his brother. "You should be thanking me, not mocking me, so knock it off."

Grumbling, Kevin began his long schlep home and Nick went to unhitch Penny. A few minutes later, Lucy appeared. Kevin was right—she was so fair her skin glowed in the moonlight, which also reflected off her glasses. It was a good thing she was carrying a bag; it served as an anchor to keep the stiff wind from carrying her away.

"Here, let me help you," Nick offered, indicating he'd assist Lucy into his open one-seat buggy.

"I can manage," she replied, using her free hand to pull herself into the carriage. But the step was too high or the bag too heavy because she faltered backward and Nick steadied her by her waist—he could practically encircle his hands around it—before giving her a clumsy boost up. She scooted to the far end of the front seat, clutching her bag to her chest as if it contained gold.

On the way Nick tried to drum up something to say, but he drew a blank. Recognizing he and Lucy had absolutely nothing in common except they were both Willow Creek Amish singles, he was relieved this charade would last only a week, or two at most.

Finally, he remarked, "I really appreciate your letting me say I'm courting you. Knowing how quickly the rumor mill spins, everyone probably saw us leave and they're already gossiping that we're getting married."

Ach! It was true their peers were probably expressing curiosity about their relationship, but why did Nick even bring up the notion of marriage? As if this experience weren't already awkward enough as it was.

Lucy giggled behind her hand. "That's not likely," she said, and Nick didn't know if she meant it wasn't likely their peers were already gossiping about them or it wasn't likely the two of them would ever get married. Of *course* the latter wasn't likely, but it was kind of haughty for her to snicker at the idea.

Lucy dropped her hand to her lap again, guarding her bag. "So when do you want to get started on the repairs?"

"As soon as possible," Nick replied, glad to switch subjects. "I can't start on Monday because I'll be returning from a trip to one of our suppliers out of town.

So I'll probably buy the stuff I need and begin the prep work on Tuesday night."

"That's fine. I'll arrange to make an early supper for my family and you can pick me up any time after six. I'll wait on the porch so Mildred and Katura won't accost you with questions."

"What?" Nick panicked, his pulse galloping. He only wanted to *imply* he was courting Lucy; he hadn't intended to actually take her out. "What do you mean, pick you up? You do realize this is a *pretend* courtship, don't you?"

Lucy didn't know whether she was amused or annoyed by Nick's alarmed reaction. It was obvious he'd never consider dating her for real. Not that she wanted him to, but still, he didn't have to act so repulsed.

"Of course I realize this is a pretend courtship. But I'm not going to lie about going out with you and I'm not going to allow you to use my name to lie about it, either. If you tell your *eldre*—if you even *imply* to them—you're spending an evening out with me, then you've got to actually spend some part of the evening out with me."

Nick gulped audibly. "You want to *kumme* with me while I work on the cabin?"

Lucy couldn't do that. The sawdust would cause her allergies to act up. "*Neh.* You can drop me off at the library and then pick me up when you're finished. That way, if anyone asks where we went—which they shouldn't, but that won't necessarily stop them—I can truthfully say you took me for a ride and we stopped at the library."

Nick hesitantly conceded, adding, "I always knew

you were a bookworm but I didn't realize you like to read quite that much. I'll be gone for a couple of hours each evening, you know."

Lucy was surprised Nick knew she liked to read—their paths hardly crossed since they had been scholars in the town's two-room schoolhouse. She'd chatted with him a few times when her cousin Bridget still lived in Willow Creek and was walking out with him, but that was almost three years ago. For some reason it annoyed Lucy that Nick called her a bookworm, the same term her stepmother used to describe her.

"It's true I like to read. Reading allows me to learn about new ideas and places. But that's not why I want you to drop me off at the library," she said. "I have a special embroidery project I need to finish by December 21 and the library is a quiet place to do that." Then, to make it clear she was as disinterested in being courted by him as he was in becoming her suitor, she said, "That's the only reason I agreed to this arrangement. Otherwise, Betty and my sisters would pressure me into attending all the upcoming *Grischtdaag* social events and I'd never finish my project on time."

"Oh, so that's why you were embroidering at the singing," Nick replied. "I just thought you were too stuck—"

Nick cut his sentence short but Lucy knew what he was going to say. He was going to call her stuck-up. She wasn't unaware some young men thought that about her, but she'd never been told it outright. Why the *meed* in Willow Creek thought Nick Burkholder was such a catch, she'd never know, but Lucy wasn't impressed by his manners.

Changing topics, she asked, "How long will it take to make the repairs?"

"I should be done in a week. Ten days, at most."

Lucy was actually hoping it would take longer than that, but she'd just have to make the most of her time away from the house. "And then what will we tell people?"

"What do you mean?"

"I'll agree to pretend we're walking out together until your repairs are finished, but not any longer than that. It would be nosy for someone to ask us why we've broken up, but in case they do, it's a *gut* idea to have a credible answer ready. After all, two weeks is an awfully short time for a courtship, even for you," she said, not mincing words.

Nick puffed loudly, as if exasperated. "I suppose we'll just say it didn't work out."

"Ha," Lucy uttered. "If you think that answer will satisfy my sisters' curiosity, you don't know how persistent they can be."

"Then what do you propose we say instead?"

Lucy was quiet. How would she know what to say? She'd never been in a real courtship, much less a phony one. "I guess we'll have to cross that bridge when we *kumme* to it."

"Yeah, all right." Nick urged his horse into a quicker trot, as if he couldn't wait to get to Lucy's house to drop her off.

She had often heard Mildred and Katura nattering on about Nick's expensive racehorse, and the animal was certainly living up to its reputation. Because it was an open-seat buggy, Lucy felt the wind biting at her cheeks as they cruised along the country roads, but she didn't mind. Despite the horse's speed, the carriage wasn't bouncing about. Lucy might not have had many conversations with men her age, but she'd read enough articles in *The Budget* to know Nick probably tinkered with the suspension of his buggy springs, which was a popular trend among Amish young people. In any case, she felt surprisingly invigorated by the quick trip home.

When they pulled up her lane, she noticed lamplight in the window. Her father would have been in bed since he worked the early shift the next day, but Betty was probably still awake. Because the step down from the carriage was higher than Lucy was used to and she had to hold on to her tote bag, she allowed Nick to assist her. Even though they were both wearing gloves, her hand warmed from the pressure of his fingers but the sensation was fleeting because he let go as soon as her feet touched the ground. Then he began walking with her to the door.

"Why are you following me?" she asked, afraid he'd want to be invited in. If Betty got one glimpse of how uncomfortable Lucy was around Nick, their cover would be blown.

"I'm not *following* you. I'm walking you to the door. You know, like I'd do if I were actually courting you," Nick explained.

Lucy's cheeks stung. Since she'd never been courted before she didn't know whether all suitors walked their girlfriends to their doors or if this was part of Nick's supposed charm.

When they reached her back porch, he loudly announced, "So I'll pick you up at six o'clock on Tuesday night, okay?"

She put her finger to her lips. "Shh! My stepmother might hear you."

Nick leaned in and whispered, "*Jah*, that's the general intention, right?" He was close enough she could smell a hint of mint chocolate cocoa on his breath and she quickly skittered up the stairs.

"*Gut nacht,*" she said over her shoulder before turning the knob to the door.

Inside Betty was sipping tea at the table and reading *The Budget*. "Hi, Lucy. I thought I heard a buggy. Are the girls stabling the horse?"

"*Neh*, they're still at the singing," Lucy answered ambiguously, avoiding meeting Betty's eyes as she removed her gloves, unwrapped her cloak and hung it on a peg by the door. She bent to unlace her boots.

"Oh? Then who brought you home?"

"Nick Burkholder," Lucy reported in what she hoped was an offhanded manner.

"Nick Burkholder?" her stepmother marveled. "Why would he bring you home? Are you sick?"

Like mamm, *like* dechder. Lucy was miffed Betty made the same assumption Mildred made about why Nick would bring her home. Lifting her chin she said, "*Neh*, I'm not sick. I'm going upstairs to bed now. *Gut nacht.*"

Lucy scurried down the hall before her stepmother could ask any more questions. The upstairs room she shared with her sisters stretched the entire length of their Cape-style home. Mildred and Katura's beds and dressers took up most of the open space, whereas Lucy's dresser and bed were tightly tucked in the back section of the room beneath the sloping roof. Because Lucy was so short, she never bumped her head on it and she liked the roof being so close to her bed. During storms, she could hear raindrops pattering the wood and she felt as if she were sleeping in an ark.

She turned on the gas lamp, sat on her bed and removed her embroidery hoop from the canvas bag. As she began unpicking her earlier mistakes, her hands trembled. She tried to tell herself it was because she'd dashed up the stairs too quickly, but she knew that wasn't it. She was breathless and quivering because Betty and her stepsisters had found it preposterous that Nick would bring her home. But what right did she have to be angry? They were correct: it was inconceivable he'd want to court her.

Yet, when she recalled his strong hands embracing her waist, the notion of a courtship didn't seem so terribly far-fetched. At least, not from her perspective. She tried to focus on restitching a delicate snowflake in the center of the napkin, but her mind kept wandering back to Nick, and after pricking her finger three times she finally gave up and went to bed.

Nick was relieved. He'd presented his proposal to Jenny, and because she'd known Nick for years, she agreed to allow him to make the repairs, provided he restored everything to its former condition by the twenty-first of December. That was her first day of winter break from the local community college and Jenny and her mother were planning to decorate the cabin together in preparation for their celebration. Based on Kevin's description of the situation, Nick assured her he didn't think it would take nearly that long, and Jenny promised she wouldn't tell anyone he was working on it.

Gripping the key to the cabin in his fist, Nick traveled to the little house in the woods, where he discovered that although the repairs were manageable, the damage was more extensive than he expected it would be. *Terrific. Now I'm going to be stuck with Lucy longer than I anticipated,* he groused.

She was already getting on his nerves, acting like he'd never read a book in his life, or as if he wanted to be invited into her house. She was so prim he couldn't imagine what they'd talk about when he was taxiing her back and forth on these so-called outings. It was a small comfort that he could count on Penny's speed to decrease their traveling time.

The entire situation was far more inconvenient and uncomfortable than Kevin knew, and Nick decided as soon as he returned home, he was going to give his brother grief—and make him fork over his paycheck for supplies, too. But when he entered the house, it was almost eleven o'clock and he was surprised to find his mother, not Kevin, sitting in the parlor.

"*Mamm?* What are you doing up?" he asked quietly.

"I'm waiting for you," she said, and rocked back and forth in her chair a few times before saying anything else. "Your brother told me where you've been."

Nick's pulse quickened—Kevin had decided to own up after all. On one hand, Nick was relieved he wouldn't have to cart Lucy back and forth to the library after all. On the other hand, he dreaded the lecture his mother was about to deliver. He straightened his posture and resigned himself to shouldering part of the blame for Kevin's carelessness in causing the fire.

"I'm surprised, but I'm glad he did."

"Well, he didn't want to, but I insisted. So don't get angry at him."

Nick was confused. Why would he be angry at Kevin for telling the truth about the fire? Before he could tell his mother he didn't understand, she said, "Don't worry. Other than telling your *daed*, I won't mention to anyone that you're courting Lucy Knepp."

Oh, right—I forgot I told Kevin to plant the seed in Mamm *and* Daed*'s minds. That's where Kevin told them I've been—at Lucy's* haus, *not at Jenny's.* Nick didn't know why but he wasn't as disappointed as he expected he'd be when he realized he'd still have to carry through with his arrangement with Lucy. Still, he was surprised his *mamm* was bringing up the topic. As often as she lectured Nick that it was time he put his running around years behind him, she rarely spoke openly about the *meed* he courted.

"*Denki,*" he said. "I appreciate that—"

His mother butted in, "Lucy Knepp is a *wunderbaar maedel.*"

Good—his mother approved. This was going to be easier than he thought. "*Jah,* she is—"

Again, his mother cut him off. "So you'd better not be up to any shenanigans."

"Wh-what do you mean?" Nick sputtered. Had Kevin let something else about their plan slip?

"She's not like other *meed* you've courted. You'd better not be toying with her feelings, *suh.*"

Nick clenched his jaw. While it was true he'd courted many *meed* who were frequently distraught when he ended their relationships, he never set out to hurt anyone's feelings. He was offended his own mother would think that was ever his intention. "I wouldn't do that,

Mamm. I wouldn't deliberately play around with any woman's emotions."

His mother must have caught the defensiveness in his voice because she said, "*Neh*, I don't suppose you would, Nick. I only mean I want you to be careful, okay? As I said, Lucy's not like other *meed* you've courted. She's…she's special."

She's special all right. She's so special she thinks she's a cut above everyone else, Nick thought. As uncomfortable as he was discussing this subject with his mother, he felt it was important to emphasize, "I've always considered *every* woman I've courted to be special."

"I believe you have, *suh*. But some women are more…they're more *earnest* than others. I don't think Lucy has had many suitors and I wouldn't want her to get her hopes up about a relationship with you if that's not a real possibility," his mother explained.

It seemed a struggle for her to find the right words, but Nick knew what she meant. She meant he'd ended every relationship he'd had so far, and she was assuming he'd end this one, too. As much as Nick resented the implication, he admitted there was an element of truth to it.

"Don't worry," he assured his mother. "I've made my intentions very clear to Lucy. But she's not quite as naive as you think. I got the feeling she was reluctant to walk out with me. We're not even really courting, it's more like we're spending time together. I'm sort of helping her with…with one of her charity endeavors for *Grischtdaag*. After that, we'll have to see what happens."

His mother looked perplexed, but she smiled and

said, "Well, for your sake, I hope it works out this time. Who knows, Lucy might be a *gut* influence on you."

That was exactly what Nick was hoping his parents would think about Lucy, but now that he heard his mother say the words, he was disgruntled. Who was to say *he* wouldn't be a good influence on *her*? Maybe he'd show her a thing or two about how to lighten up and be a little more social. Didn't anyone ever consider that?

Mildred and Katura were considerate enough not to turn on the lamp while they were getting ready for bed, but their voices woke Lucy anyway.

"I wish Mark didn't have to go back to Ohio tomorrow morning," Mildred whined. "One of the rare few likable guys who comes to Willow Creek leaves as soon as he gets here. It's not fair. I hope he visits Frederick again at *Grischtdaag*."

"Speaking of Frederick, didn't you tell me he was planning to ask to court Lucy tonight?"

"That's what Melinda Schrock told me she heard Frederick's mother saying to Jesse's *ant* in the store last week," Mildred said, and her words caused Lucy to remember what the book of James said about a little fire kindling a great matter.

"Do you think Frederick got a chance to ask to court Lucy before she left with Nick?" Katura questioned.

"Probably not. Otherwise, she would have stayed until the singing was over so Frederick could have given her a ride home. Or she would have asked him for a ride right then since she was sick."

"I suppose that's true." Katura yawned. "Can you

believe she asked Nick for a ride instead? That's awfully forward."

"*Jah*, but Nick's so nice he probably agreed because he felt sorry for her."

Lucy considered coughing to let her stepsisters know she was awake and could hear them, but she felt too humiliated. Why didn't Mildred and Katura believe she hadn't left because she was ill? Couldn't they at least *entertain* the possibility Nick was interested in her?

As if answering Lucy's unspoken question, Katura said, "One thing's for sure. He'd never consider being her suitor. She's not his type. Nick only courts women who are outgoing and adventuresome. You know, women who are more like you and me."

Lucy heard Mildred gasp. "That's it!" she exclaimed. "Nick probably wanted to talk to Lucy about one of us!"

"Do you really think so?" Katura questioned, and Lucy discerned the hopeful catch in her voice.

"*Jah*. That's how *buwe* in Willow Creek sometimes determine if a *maedel* is interested in being courted. They talk to her friends or sisters. Or if they're really shy, they'll pass a note," Mildred explained knowingly.

"But Nick isn't shy at all."

"*Neh*, not usually. But maybe he likes one of us so much he's afraid we'll reject him. Maybe that's why it's taken him so long to propose courtship—he hasn't been able to work up the courage. So instead of asking us straight out, he's taking the safe approach."

Lucy would have been inflamed, but instead she pushed her quilt against her mouth to suppress a giggle. Her stepsisters might have lacked self-awareness, but they sure didn't lack self-esteem.

"*I* should get him. I'm the oldest," Katura demanded, as if she were competing for a prize.

"You can't claim him. He'll decide for himself which one of us he wants to court."

As her stepsisters bickered about who was more worthy to have Nick as her suitor, Lucy rolled to her side and curled the pillow over her ear to block them out. They may have been right to think Nick didn't want to court Lucy, but they were just as wrong to imagine he wanted to court either of them. Once again, she stifled a guffaw. She couldn't wait for her cousin Bridget to visit at Christmastime so they could share a laugh over the hilarious irony of it all.

Chapter Three

Lucy woke early on Monday morning, planning to make breakfast for her father before he left for work. Betty and her daughters weren't early risers, so Lucy cherished the time she had alone with her *daed*. It was one of the rare occasions when she could get a word in edgewise, but sometimes instead of conversing they ate in companionable silence, enjoying the familiarity of the pattern they'd established years before Betty and the girls moved in. But by the time Lucy dressed, brushed her long hair into a bun and washed her face, she heard the wheels of a car rolling down the lane.

The Amish weren't allowed to drive or own automobiles, but they were permitted to accept rides from *Englischers*. Lucy's father's colleague, Ray, routinely picked him up since their house was on the way to the woodworking production company where they were employed. Not one to take a neighbor's generosity for granted, Lucy's father regularly assisted Ray with significant house and yard projects such as roofing or installing fencing.

Marvin just as well could have taken the buggy to

work, but Lucy had an inkling he wanted to be sure there was transportation at home for her. For one thing, if she needed to deliver her goods to Schrock's Shop, her father didn't like her to walk, even though Main Street was barely a mile away. For another, Lucy knew he secretly wanted to ensure there was a way for someone to seek medical intervention quickly in the event she developed breathing problems. Two years ago she suffered an acute respiratory attack while she and Betty were at home without a buggy. Betty had had to run to the phone shanty to call for help, and she had wound up gasping so bad by the time the ambulance arrived that the paramedics thought *she* was the patient. The episode had shaken Lucy's father deeply, and after that he always left the buggy behind.

Touched by her father's thoughtfulness, Lucy never let him know that most days it was Mildred or Katura who used the buggy to travel the short distance to their jobs on Main Street, where they worked part-time. They were both cashiers at the mercantile, which was a grocery and goods store catering primarily to Willow Creek's Amish. Granted, the two young women spent the better part of their shift on their feet, but most Amish *meed* in their area walked farther than that to get to their jobs.

When the two of them weren't using the buggy, Betty was. She frequently journeyed to Elmsville to visit her ailing sister. But Lucy never cared; she was so glad to have some quiet time to herself she would have offered to carry her stepsisters to town on her back if it meant she didn't have to listen to their prattle.

That's a very judgmental thing for me to think, she reflected. *The Lord makes us all different. I don't like them criticizing me for keeping to myself so I shouldn't criticize them for being so chatty.*

Since she was awake and dressed anyway, Lucy decided she'd make breakfast for the other women. They loved buttermilk pancakes and sausage, and a hot breakfast would hit the spot before they set out in the chilly November air. She set four places at the table, and just after she ladled the last scoop of batter onto the iron griddle, Mildred and Katura appeared in the doorway.

"That smells *appenditlich*," Mildred gushed.

"But you shouldn't have gone to the trouble. Especially not after being sick last night," Katura protested, showing a rare concern for Lucy's health.

"It's not a bother and, as I told you, I wasn't ill," she insisted as Betty ambled into the room.

"Guder mariye," she greeted the three young women. "What a treat to have *pannekuche* and *wascht*. What's the special occasion? Did something happen last night you want to tell us about?"

Lucy was taken aback by how blatantly Betty hinted she wanted to know more about why Nick had brought her home. Despite the fact most Willow Creek Amish youth kept their courtships to themselves, it was clear to Lucy this was one more way in which her stepsisters and stepmother abided by a different set of customs than Lucy did. She could never figure out if the difference was a matter of their personalities or if it was because they were from the Elmsville district, which was governed by a slightly more lenient *Ordnung*.

"Jah, something *did* happen last night!" Mildred blurted out. "Nick Burkholder left the singing early to give Lucy a ride home. And we think we know why."

Even though Betty was already aware Nick had brought Lucy home, she raised an eyebrow and asked, "Why?"

"He wants to court either Mildred or me. Probably me," Katura said. Then she demanded, "Out with it, Lucy. Did he give you a message to give one of us?"

It was one thing for Katura and Mildred to whisper about their theories when they thought she was asleep, but Lucy was dumbfounded they'd suggest right to her face Nick had brought her home only to inquire about them. No wonder they'd been so solicitous about her making breakfast—they were trying to flatter her. Maybe they were each hoping she'd put in a good word for them with Nick.

"*Neh*, he didn't mention either of you at all," she said, sounding as complacent as she felt. She slid the final pancakes onto a platter. After placing the dish on the table, she sat down and asked, "Shall I say grace?"

No sooner had she finished thanking the Lord for their food and asking Him to bless their day than Mildred coaxed, "You probably don't want to make one of us feel bad, but we can't stand not knowing who Nick's interested in. Please tell us, Lucy."

Betty cleared her throat. "They're right, Lucy. It isn't fair of you to keep the girls on tenterhooks like this."

That was the last straw. "Okay, if you must know," Lucy began, and Mildred leaned forward while Katura froze with her fork midair. "It's *me* he's interested in spending time with. In fact, he's picking me up at six o'clock on Tuesday evening."

Katura lowered her utensil and Mildred slouched back against her chair again. Lucy almost felt sorry she'd crushed their hopes until Mildred waved her hand dismissively and said, "Okay then, don't tell us the truth. We'll find out eventually."

"But she *has* to tell us which one of us he wants to court," Katura contradicted. "What if she convinces him I'm not interested? Or that you're not interested? I don't want her speaking on my behalf, do you?"

"Lucy, you can't—" Mildred began to whine.

To Lucy's surprise, Betty broke in. "If Lucy says Nick is interested in her, I think that's nice, so stop pestering her. You two girls will have plenty of opportunities to socialize with all the *Grischtdaag* parties and events coming up anyway." She reached over and patted Lucy's hand and said, "Don't worry, I'll tell your *daed* about your new suitor. As long as you finish your household chores each day, I'm sure he won't mind if you walk out with Nick at night."

Lucy wanted to retort that she always finished her chores and half of her stepsisters' chores, too, but she was so grateful Betty had put an end to Mildred and Katura's needling she let the remark slide.

At least that part of the plan is accomplished, she thought. She couldn't help but wonder if Nick was having as much difficulty convincing his family they were courting as she'd had convincing hers.

It was easier for Nick to get out of working late on Tuesday than he expected. Apparently, his mother had told his father he was courting Lucy, and there were no objections when he asked if there was any way he could leave work at his usual time that week.

"No problem. Kevin and I can manage things here," his father said, clapping Nick on the shoulder. Apparently, he thought as highly of Lucy as Nick's mother did.

As Nick was leaving, Kevin smirked and whispered, "Have a *gut* time. And remember, this is temporary. Don't break Lucy's delicate little heart." Then he puckered his mouth and smacked his lips in an exaggerated kissing gesture.

"Don't start anything on fire," Nick retorted as he set his hat on his head and exited through the back door.

When he turned down the lane to Lucy's house, he spotted her standing on the porch, clutching a cloak around her chest. It wasn't *that* cold outside, but she was behaving as if it were ten degrees below zero. He hoped she wasn't going to complain about riding in an open-seat buggy in this weather.

He hopped down from the carriage while she crossed the yard in the light streaming from the house windows. "Hi, Lucy," he said, and reached to support her as she climbed into the buggy, but she kept her arms snug around her chest. *She acts as if we're still* kinner *in school and I have the cooties*, he thought.

"Hello, Nick," she said in a hushed tone. "Don't look toward the window because I think we have an audience. I'm hiding my embroidery materials beneath my cloak. I don't want Betty and my stepsisters to see, because they might realize we're not actually walking out together."

Nick chuckled. So she wasn't as standoffish as he'd thought. "It's already too dark for them to see this far. They'll never know. But here, let me help."

He cupped Lucy's elbow to propel her upward, but she was so light he nearly tossed her into the buggy and she flung her arms out for balance, upending her tote bag.

"My linen!" she wailed as she retrieved a rectangle of fabric white enough to see in the twilight. "I hope it didn't get dirty."

"Sorry about that," he apologized, feeling like a bull in a china shop. Usually his confidence wasn't so easily rattled.

They didn't say another word until they were nearly at the library and Nick asked, "What are you going to say if someone sees you in the library?"

"I'll probably say hello."

Nick looked at her sideways, but he couldn't discern from her profile if she was joking or if she was just too obtuse to know what he meant. "*Neh*, I mean what excuse are you going to give them for being there alone?"

"Why do I need an excuse to be at the library alone? It's not as if anyone other than our families know we're supposedly going out together tonight, right? Your family will be busy at the store and mine wouldn't dream of coming to the library. So if I meet anyone else from our district, I'll simply greet them as usual."

Nick was dubious. He knew how quickly rumors spread in Willow Creek, especially when *meed* like Katura and Mildred were involved. If they told their peers Nick and Lucy were walking out that night and then someone saw Lucy alone, it wouldn't take long before their farce would be discovered.

"Do you suppose you could keep a low profile anyway?" he requested.

"Unfortunately, a low profile is all I can keep." Lucy giggled. "Let's just say being five feet tall is something of a *shortcoming*."

Amused, Nick smiled. Most *meed* he courted were too self-conscious to laugh at what they considered physical imperfections. Not that Lucy's height was an imperfection—it was how the Lord had created her— but she was unusually short compared to most of the Amish in their district.

In the library parking lot he offered to help her down from the carriage, but she insisted she could manage on her own. Covertly glancing around, he noticed a group of *Englisch* preteen girls hanging out on the library steps—probably waiting for their parents—but he didn't see any Amish people or buggies. "I'll be back at eight thirty to pick you up," he said.

"The library doesn't close until nine so it's fine if you're running a few minutes late." When Lucy smiled Nick noticed that her straight, white teeth gleamed in the light cast by the streetlamp. He watched as she trod past the *Englischers* who gave her a once-over and then giggled behind their hands. Not even as tall as the shortest of the girls, Lucy held her head high and swung her canvas bag as she passed them. Whether she was oblivious to their presence or deliberately ignoring their ridicule, Nick couldn't guess. Lucy was more complicated than she seemed on the surface, a characteristic he found both intriguing and frustrating.

Nick directed his horse toward an *Englisch* lumberyard in Highland Springs. Ordinarily, he would have purchased his supplies from the local lumberyard, but the *Englisch* one was open late and he was relatively certain he wouldn't see anyone he knew there at this time of evening.

Since he'd already made Kevin purchase most of the supplies he'd need from their father's hardware store, Nick only needed to buy paneling. It was a challenge to secure the long pieces of wood in his courting buggy, and he frequently had to stop along the way to the cabin to reposition them.

As he journeyed, Nick thought about Kevin grumbling over how much the supplies cost. That should have been the least of his brother's concerns. It was as if the boy didn't fully appreciate how much trouble he would have been in if Jenny Nelson hadn't extended such grace. Nick asked the Lord to touch Kevin's conscience and to open his eyes to his careless behavior. *Please,* Gott, *help me to be a better example to him, too.*

When he arrived at the cabin, he flicked on the lights and began unloading the supplies. Preoccupied with trying to figure out where to begin deconstructing the wall, Nick didn't realize how late it was until a clock chimed eight times—or was it nine? He glanced at the mantel place clock. It was nine. The library was closed and Lucy would be waiting. Experience told him the only thing worse than breaking up with a woman was being late for one. She was going to be madder than a hornet.

He flung the last of the materials into a messy stack in the corner of the room, locked the cabin door and bounded across the lawn to his buggy. This was one of the many occasions when it was clear that buying Penny hadn't been an impractical choice; the animal trotted as quickly as Nick allowed and he arrived at the library within fifteen minutes.

As he approached the building he couldn't see Lucy and he worried she may have left without him. But how? From what he could tell, it wasn't likely she'd undertake a walk that far in daytime, much less in the dark. His heart shuddered. Had something befallen her? But when he scanned the entrance area again, he spotted her partially obscured by shrubbery on the side of the library steps. Her bag was at her side and she was sitting with her arms wrapped around her knees. *She's so thin she's probably chilled to the bone*, he thought.

Her head was tilted toward the sky and Nick wondered if she was praying. Maybe she was asking God to hasten Nick's arrival. He brought his buggy to a halt and jumped down. His movement seemed to startle her, and she rose and absentmindedly brushed off her skirt.

"I'm sorry, Lucy," he said. "I got so involved with my tasks I entirely lost track of time."

Still looking upward, she replied, "I understand how that can happen. I was so absorbed in my embroidery I almost got locked inside the library just now. The librarian found me in a corner chair in the basement and chased me out. Look, is that Mars?"

Astounded that Lucy wasn't angry, Nick's eyes followed the skyward direction of her pointed finger. "*Jah*, I think you're right."

"It's beautiful, isn't it?" she asked. "I'm usually not outside at this time of night so I hardly ever get to see the planets and the stars."

Nick saw them all the time, but he never stopped to appreciate them the way she apparently did. They stood side by side in silence observing the sky until a shiver passed over Lucy and she said, "We'd better get going. It's late."

Reluctantly, Nick nodded and reached for her bag. He repeated his apology. "I really am sorry I wasn't here when I said I'd be here. It won't happen again."

This time he assisted her into the buggy more gingerly than he had the first time, and instead of handing her the wool blanket he kept in the buggy, he spread it across her lap and tucked it beneath her feet with care.

Lucy had the sensation she was floating. She tried to convince herself it was because she'd made so much progress on her stitching, but that wasn't the only reason. The truth was, she liked the idea of being courted, even if it was a false courtship. The experience of being outdoors at night beneath the stars was romantic in itself, and no man except her father had ever assisted her into and out of a buggy. She'd been missing out. If the attentiveness of a young man who wasn't even a real suitor made her feel this blissful, how might she feel if the man truly liked her? Maybe when her stint with Nick was completed, she should accept Frederick as a suitor after all. She still couldn't really picture it, but then she never imagined a buggy ride with Nick Burkholder could be so pleasant, either.

"You're home late," Mildred commented. She and Katura were lounging across their beds, but they hadn't yet turned off the lamp when Lucy entered the bedroom. "Where did you and Nick go?"

"Oh, we went…out," Lucy replied vaguely.

Katura tossed her long, loose hair over her shoulder, clearly pretending to be indifferent. "Could you turn down the lamp, please?" she asked. "Some of us have to go to work in the morning."

It was a barb that ordinarily would have gotten Lucy's goat. She worked just as hard as her stepsisters did to contribute to their family's expenses, and she dared say she worked harder on keeping house. Furthermore, since Betty regularly visited her sister in Elmsville, most of the meal preparation fell to Lucy, too. But tonight she shrugged off the comment and dimmed the light as requested.

The room was quiet and by the time she eased into her bed, Lucy thought her stepsisters had fallen asleep. But then Mildred urgently hissed, "Spill the beans already, Lucy. What did you and Nick do tonight?"

A delicious vibration fluttered down Lucy's spine as she said, "We went for a ride and we talked."

Katura snorted, belying her earlier indifference. "That doesn't sound like very much *schpass*. Or very romantic."

"We also looked at the scars in the sty," Lucy bashfully confided.

"The scars in the sty? Don't you mean the *stars in the sky*?" Katura shrieked. She and Mildred laughed uproariously and Lucy's face felt scalding hot. She couldn't account for the slip of her tongue, but now her stepsisters were going to think she was so smitten with Nick she couldn't speak straight. "I must be overly tired," she said by way of excuse, and quickly joined in with their laughter so they wouldn't know how abashed she was by her mistake.

After they quieted down, Mildred pried, "Did it seem like he wants to take you out again sometime?"

"*Jah.* We're getting together on Thursday night."

"That soon?" Katura sounded surprised. Then she added nonchalantly, "I suppose that's all right, as long as he's able to attend our caroling rehearsal on Friday night. We're going out for pizza afterward."

It irritated Lucy that Katura acted as if she were granting permission for Nick to court her, but she didn't want to say anything in her defense, lest she trip over her words again. So Lucy simply bade her stepsisters good-night and pulled her quilt up to her chin.

She slept so soundly she realized upon waking she had missed another opportunity to prepare her father breakfast. And by the time Lucy was dressed, Katura and Mildred had already left for work, too. It must have been all that fresh air the night before—she never slept this late. Now she was going to have to hurry to make up for lost time. She had to complete a Christmas tree skirt she was custom designing for a customer from Schrock's by this afternoon so she could drop it off at the shop on the way to the soup kitchen that evening.

In the kitchen she discovered a note from Betty indicating she'd be spending the day with her indisposed sister again. She requested that Lucy prepare supper and instructed Mildred and Katura to sweep the floors and beat the rugs when they returned home. Lucy tried not to think ungracious thoughts, but preparing supper took longer than beating the rugs and sweeping the floors, especially since those tasks would be shared between the two sisters. Lucy didn't usually mind doing housework—in fact, she preferred the house being neater and more organized than the others did—but today she desperately needed time to work on the tree skirt.

Once she'd chopped vegetables and cubed the meat for stew, she put them in a pot to simmer throughout the day. Then she began making bread. In between kneading the dough, punching it down and allowing it to rise again, she embroidered the final touches on the tree skirt. With its array of pine trees and cardinals, church bells and candy canes, the design was exactly what the customer wanted, although it was too flashy for Lucy's taste. She preferred the simplicity of white-on-white snowflakes or perhaps the accent of a sprig of holly here and there.

Like their linens and curtains, the Amish tended to keep their house decorations simple, too, but Lucy relished the Christmas holiday season when she could place candles on the windowsills and arrange evergreen boughs on the mantel. It didn't take much to make their home feel festive and Lucy couldn't wait to begin adorning it on Saturday. Perhaps this year Katura and Mildred would help her. *I'll probably have to bribe them with cocoa and cookies though.* Immediately she regretted her sour thought and she asked God to forgive her attitude.

Mildred once asked Lucy if she got bored "sitting around embroidering all day," but Lucy seldom did. Not only did she enjoy creating freehand designs, but she also used the time to pray. For example, as she worked on the Christmas tree skirt, she prayed that the family who ordered it would have a healthy, joyful, Christ-centered time of worship together.

Then her mind drifted to Nick. Reflecting on his willingness to help repair the cabin for Christmas, she realized she wouldn't have guessed he'd demonstrate such a selfless devotion to his *Englisch* friend. Thinking of him, she was tickled by a chill, and she rose to stoke the stove and check on the stew.

By the time her stepmother and sisters came home, it was four o'clock. Her father returned at four thirty. He knew how important it was for Lucy to work at the soup kitchen, so he always made a point to return home by four thirty on Wednesdays, even if it meant he had to walk whenever his *Englisch* coworker was putting in overtime and couldn't give him a lift home. This was one of those days.

"*Denki* for walking home, *Daed*," she told him after she'd dropped the skirt off at Schrock's and they were on their way to the soup kitchen. She was perfectly capable of handling the buggy herself, but he insisted, so she let him. It was another cherished occasion when she could spend time with him alone.

"What you do at the soup kitchen is important," he said. "Just don't let yourself get too run-down. Now that you're...you're socializing more, you might not have as much energy as you usually do."

Lucy caught her father's profile in her peripheral vision. Although he used the term "socializing" instead of "courting," she felt guilty. Grinning broadly, he appeared so pleased. "I'm not actually..." she began, but then she realized she couldn't back out of her agreement with Nick. It meant so much to him—and to the Nelsons. "I'm not going to get too run-down, *Daed*."

"*Gut*. Because you deserve to enjoy yourself. And any young man—er, any young person who keeps company with such a smart, engaging *maedel* like you is very fortunate."

Lucy was touched by how careful her father was to avoid using Nick's name, as well as by his endearing sentiments. She knew few men in Willow Creek besides her father would consider her to be engaging, but she appreciated his opinion all the same.

At the church where the soup kitchen was located, Dan Ebersole was retrieving folding chairs from the closet near the back door where Lucy entered the building. Having recently moved from an Amish settlement in Ohio to nearby Elmsville and being reserved by nature, Dan didn't have many friends, but he and Lucy had struck it off well together. "Your face is... It's kind of glowing," he faltered. "I mean, you look really happy tonight."

"I *am* really happy," she said. "It must be because *Grischtdaag* is my favorite holiday and it's getting closer." But as much as she loved Christmas, Lucy had never felt quite this cheerful about the holiday before. No, this kind of joy came from somewhere else.

On Thursday evening before starting off for Lucy's house, Nick asked his mother for another wool blanket to stow in his buggy.

"Is there a snowstorm on the horizon?" she asked with a lilt in her voice.

"*Neh*, I want it in case Lucy gets cold," he answered before he realized his mother was teasing him. His ears blazing, he hurried from the house.

As he directed Penny across town, he reasoned it was only common sense to bring an extra blanket for Lucy. She was so thin the wind probably went right through her, and he didn't want her to complain. Then he began to worry that Lucy, like his mother, might interpret the gesture as something other than his being considerate; she might interpret it as a sign of affection. He couldn't have that. This was a phony, short-term courtship, nothing more. So after Lucy was seated in the buggy, Nick handed her the spare folded blanket instead of arranging it for her as he'd done on Tuesday evening.

"The library again?" he asked tersely.

"*Jah*, please," she replied.

A long silence followed until he grew restless and

finally thought to inquire about her project. Her voice was animated as she described the soup kitchen and how the organization needed to raise at least one thousand dollars in order to repair their commercial-sized oven and cover other expenses associated with their service.

"Lately the soup kitchen should be called a sandwich and cookie kitchen, since we aren't able to serve hot meals." Lucy sighed. "I feel so bad because this is the time of year when people need something to warm their bellies more than ever."

Nick had had no idea her embroidering project was for the soup kitchen's benefit; he had assumed she was making it to sell for a profit. At best, he'd imagined she'd use the proceeds to buy Christmas presents for her family, but he hadn't considered she was working this hard to give the money away to charity. "That's really generous of you, donating your time and skills to the soup kitchen like that," he said.

She dipped her head modestly. "It's no more generous than what you're doing—using your skills to help someone else have a merry *Grischtdaag*."

Nick felt a pinch of guilt. There was a world of difference between what he was doing and what she was doing, even if she wasn't aware of it. "It's not a big deal," he said.

"Oh, but it is." She twisted toward him. "I've heard how much you like to socialize, and at this time of year there are so many parties and events going on that you're forfeiting just to help your friend's family— *Englischers* at that."

So she was also aware of how much he liked to socialize. Was Nick's brother right about his reputation preceding him? Or did she get that idea from someone else, like her cousin Bridget, whom he had once courted? Nick wondered what else Lucy had heard about him—specifically, about his courtships.

"Speaking of parties," he said. "As you probably know, there's a get-together on Friday night after the caroling rehearsal. I planned to work on the cabin, but if you're going to the party, then…"

Lucy picked up his sentence where he left off. "Then we'd have to go together?"

"Neh!" he exclaimed. "I didn't mean that. I meant if you're going to the party then I can't tell people I'm with you on Friday night because obviously they'll see you alone at the party."

"Oh, right. Of course," Lucy said. Nick couldn't read her tone for certain, but he got the sense he had offended her.

"Unless you wanted to go to the party," he offered guiltily. "I mean, if that's the case I should probably go with you. For the sake of appearances."

Lucy sat up straighter and shook her head. *"Neh,* definitely not. I mean, I don't want to go to the party with or without you, so it's fine if you work on the cabin. You can pick me up at the usual time."

"But isn't the library closed on Friday evening?"

"Jah, but there's a little bookstore café that's open until nine thirty or ten down the street from the library. I could do my embroidery there."

"You really wouldn't mind?" Nick couldn't believe how flexible she was being. Was she doing that just for him? He felt torn between wishing she was and hoping she wasn't.

"I'd consider it a favor," she said. "Otherwise, Betty

will insist I go to the party and that will set me back on my embroidery."

Oh, so that was why. Nick should have known. "*Denki*, that would be great," he replied. But if the idea was so agreeable to him, why did he feel so let down?

Chapter Four

After working on her project three evenings during the week, as well as on Saturday evening after she'd decorated their home for Christmas, Lucy began to relax a little about her deadline. It was only the fourth of December; she had until the twenty-first to finish. By the Sabbath, she was almost relieved to take a break. It was an "off Sunday," which meant instead of gathering for church, the Amish families in Willow Creek held worship services in their individual homes. Afterward, the family enjoyed a light dinner of cheese sandwiches and chicken soup, and then everyone either read or napped. Except for Lucy—she pulled out a pen and paper to write to her cousin.

> Dear Bridget,
> It's less than three more weeks until you visit and I can't wait to see you again! Be sure to bring your ice skates—the weather here is unseasonably cold and if it keeps up, we'll be able to skate on Wheeler's Pond.

Although Lucy often got winded when she exerted herself in the cold weather, she and Bridget both loved to skate. Lucy had better balance but Bridget was faster, so they helped each other navigate the home-made outdoor rink at the local pond, which was often crowded with both *Englisch* and Amish skaters and ice hockey players. It was rare for the pond to freeze over at Christmastime; usually they had to wait until January or February, so Lucy was delighted to think she and Bridget might be able to go skating the way they used to before her cousin moved away.

Chewing on the end of her pen, Lucy pondered whether she should tell Bridget about her arrangement with Nick, and if so, what she should say. What had begun as an opportunity to complete her project had turned into... Well, Lucy wasn't sure what it had turned into, but she wasn't as eager to share the details of the arrangement with Bridget as she was when she thought they'd share a good laugh over the irony of it.

Am I worried what she'd say if I told her Nick is nothing like I thought he was? Lucy wondered. Truthfully, she had to admit that was part of her hesitation. Lucy knew Bridget had experienced Nick's duplicitous behavior firsthand and, out of protectiveness toward her cousin, Bridget would warn Lucy about his cunning ways. But Lucy didn't need a warning because she wasn't going to become involved in a romantic relationship with Nick. She was simply enjoying his company more than she expected she would.

Which was a good thing, considering Nick told her his project was going to take longer than expected—perhaps more than two weeks. It had something to do with the drywall or plasterboard behind the paneling, as she vaguely recalled. In any case, Lucy would probably finish the tablecloth and napkins before he finished the walls. If that happened, she'd put an end to their arrangement... Wouldn't she?

"Lucy!" Katura startled her. "Didn't you hear me?"

"She was daydreaming about *N-i-c-k*," Mildred teased, just like a schoolgirl.

Lucy hadn't heard them enter the room. "I'm sorry, I was thinking about Bridget. What did you say?" she asked.

"We've planned a caroling rehearsal for tonight at Melinda and Jesse Schrock's *haus*. I know you're not participating in the caroling, but we're only going to practice for half an hour and then we're going to break for games and snacks. Do you want to *kumme*?"

Even though Melinda and Jesse were already married, the couple frequently hosted groups of young single adults at their home and Melinda was nicknamed "Melinda Matchmaker," a title she reveled in.

"*Denki*, but I've been out a lot this week."

"There's no need to boast. A simple *neh* would suffice," Mildred said, rolling her eyes.

"I only meant I'm tired. I want to catch up on my letter writing."

Katura sat down across the table from Lucy and leaned forward. "Did you and Nick have an argument?" she whispered.

"*Neh*. I'm just tired and I don't want to go out. I want to go to bed early this evening."

Before she finished speaking, Lucy's father walked into the room. "Then that's exactly what you should do," he said, donning his coat before going to milk the cows for the evening. "It's too cold outside for Lucy. But if you want to go out tonight, Mildred and Katura, I'll hitch the buggy for you."

While Lucy appreciated her father's concern, as well as his attempt to thwart her stepsisters' badgering, she didn't want his overprotectiveness about her health today to interfere with her plans to go out with Nick later in the week since the temperatures were forecasted to drop even further. Plus—she hated to admit it to herself—it occurred to her belatedly Nick might be at the rehearsal, too.

"It's not that cold, *Daed*," she said, changing her mind about attending the singing. "Actually, now that I think of it, I've been cooped up inside all day and I'd like to go."

Her father opened his mouth, but Lucy shot him a pleading look, knowing he wouldn't protest when she added, "Even if I'm not going to be one of the carolers, listening to the singing always puts me in a festive mood. You know how I love *Grischtdaag*."

"Take an extra blanket then," her father advised. Having gotten her way, Lucy leaped up to wrap her arms around his midsection. Sometimes she felt as manipulative as her stepsisters. "And don't stay out late."

"We won't," Lucy promised. "We'll be home before ten."

Mildred grumbled, "Ten? Speak for yourself!" But then when Marvin narrowed his eyes she quickly suggested. "I mean, if you want to get home by ten, I'm sure Nick will take you."

"I don't even know if he'll be there." The very possibility Nick might be present caused Lucy to flush, and she looked away as she gathered her writing materials and left the room to wash her face and put on a clean dress, just in case he was.

Nick recognized it was prideful to wish he had a better singing voice, but since he was stuck with the voice he had, he figured it was better not to sing at all. Which didn't mean he was going to miss the caroling rehearsal on Sunday night. Melinda and Jesse Schrock were hosting, which meant there was sure to be a boisterous party with lots of good food after the carolers practiced their songs.

But the party wasn't the main reason he wanted to attend. He wanted to go, firstly, because he loved to exercise Penny at every opportunity. The animal seemed to enjoy it as well, zooming along at a smooth, swift pace. Some horses you had to urge onward, but Penny was the opposite, and more often Nick had to keep her from breaking into a hard run.

Secondly, he hoped Jesse might have invited Hunter Schwartz and possibly Fletcher Chupp. Although both of the men were married, Jesse and Melinda often opened their home to both singles and married couples, claiming the bigger the party the better. Fletcher was a carpenter and Hunter restored furniture, and Nick needed input about his project from both of them. The paneling he had removed from the wall was high quality wood, and while he had managed to salvage about half of it, Nick wanted to ask Hunter about staining the new pieces so they matched the original color. He also hoped Fletcher would give him advice about the drywall behind the paneling, which was in considerably worse shape than the paneling itself.

"Aren't you afraid you'll see Lucy there?" Kevin asked when Nick told him he was going to the rehearsal.

Afraid? No. It was more like he was…hopeful. In fact, the hope of seeing Lucy was one more reason Nick had decided to attend the gathering.

"She probably won't be there," he said nonchalantly. "But if she is, then she is."

"But you said those sisters of hers know you're supposedly courting her."

"So what?"

"So won't it seem strange that you didn't offer to take her to the singing?"

"*Neh.* Lots of couples are discreet about their relationships."

Kevin chuckled. "*Jah,* but you're not. Or even if you are, most of the time your peers seem to know if and who you're courting. If you show up separately from Lucy, her sisters are never going to believe you're her suitor."

Nick hadn't really thought of the fact Mildred and Katura would be there scrutinizing his presence, but Kevin was probably right. "I don't know. If Lucy's there, maybe I'll take her home afterward or something. That should put their suspicion to rest," he said. As he said it, he smiled, realizing it gave him the perfect excuse to be alone with Lucy again.

He couldn't describe how he felt about the past week except to admit it had been far more pleasant than he'd expected. He enjoyed being alone with Lucy. Talking to her. Picking her up and dropping her off. It had become a routine, and even though he saw her the previous night and had plans to pick her up on Monday evening, he found himself longing to see her again on Sunday, too.

But when he got to the Schrocks' house, there was no sign of her. Nor of Hunter or Fletcher. There was, however, a tall, curvaceous blonde woman Melinda introduced as her closest childhood friend, Eve, from Ohio.

"Eve is staying with us until the *Nei Yaahr*, isn't that right, Eve?" Melinda said.

Eve flashed her dimples, saying, "Unless Jesse gets tired of having two women gabbing in the *haus* all day and sends me home early."

If Eve is as gossipy as Melinda, I wouldn't blame him if he did, Nick thought, glancing at the door to see who just entered. The room was so crowded he couldn't get a good look over the heads of the people standing closest to him.

"I was telling Eve about Penny," Melinda continued. "Eve's *daed* trains horses for the *Englisch*, so she knows a lot about them."

"Not a lot. But I do like to help my *daed* break them in. The wilder the better, the bigger the challenge," Eve said. "Although from what Melinda tells me, they're probably not as fast as Penny."

"Nick, why don't you take Eve out for a ride?" Melinda suggested.

Ordinarily, Nick might have appreciated Melinda's obvious attempt to pair him with a newcomer to Willow Creek. That was what he'd been praying for, to meet someone new. And someone new who liked fast horses—Nick had never thought to pray for that quality in a woman, so he should have been ecstatic. Yet there was nothing about Eve that drew him in. If anything, her association with Melinda worked against her.

"I'll probably be leaving soon. I was only dropping

in for your famous brownies," he said, hoping his flattery would appease Melinda. It didn't.

"Then take her now. We'll start singing soon, and Eve's voice is as wretched as yours is, so she doesn't mind if she misses the carols," Melinda countered.

Eve blinked rapidly, clearly mortified by Melinda's put-down. Either that or Eve was as consternated by Melinda's insistence Nick take Eve for a ride as he was. In an attempt to ease both of their discomfort, Nick joked, "Let's go, Eve. We don't have to put up with Melinda's insults."

He gestured toward the door, figuring the sooner he got the ride with Eve over, the sooner he could leave. He led the way, bypassing the other guests, who bunched together balancing cups of cider and paper plates of brownies and cookies in their hands.

"It's a beautiful night for a ride," Eve commented when they stepped out onto the porch.

Nick was about to reply when he noticed movement in the dark a few feet from the porch.

A moment later, Mildred and Katura came into view. Terrific, now what was he going to do?

"Uh, hello, Mildred. H-hi, Katura," he stuttered as they climbed the stairs.

They froze, staring at him. Then a voice from behind them said, "Keep moving, please, I'm freezing." Lucy was so short her stepsisters blocked her from view, but Nick recognized her voice the second she spoke and his pulse bounded through his veins.

Lucy was impatient. It was just like Mildred and Katura to dillydally on the porch in the wintry air instead of going into the house's warm interior. When they didn't move forward, she swerved around them, nearly bumping into a blonde woman she'd never seen before. Nick was standing next to her.

"Oh, hello, Nick," she said awkwardly.

Nick cleared his throat. "Er, hi, Lucy. Have you met Melinda's friend, Eve?" He gestured to the woman at his side. "She's visiting until the *Nei Yaahr.*"

Lucy forced a smile. Her stepsisters were uncharacteristically silent, but she could feel their eyes on her. "*Wilkom* to Willow Creek, Eve," she said nonchalantly.

"*Denki.* I'm glad to be here. Everyone in this district is so friendly," she said. "Nick's even agreed to take me out for a ride in his buggy, since neither of us has a *gut* singing voice."

Katura made a coughing sound and Lucy's eyes smarted. So that was it? Nick was courting Eve now and Lucy's arrangement with him had ended, just like that? He could have at least had the decency to tell her before tonight. Now she looked like a fool in front of her stepsisters. *I should have known anyone who would court a second woman before he'd broken up with Bridget wouldn't think twice about courting a second woman before he ended a fake relationship with me.*

"Eve's *daed* trains horses for the *Englisch,*" Nick explained. "So she's an expert. She wanted to see Penny."

Lucy's tone was as cool as glass. "Well, don't let us keep you." She began moving around Nick, but he reached out and grabbed her arm near the elbow.

"Do you want to *kumme* with us?" he asked.

Baffled, Lucy didn't know what to think. If Nick was interested in Eve, why would he want Lucy to ride with them? But if he wasn't interested in Eve, why was he taking her riding alone? Either way, there was one thing she knew for certain: she didn't want to be within five miles of Nick Burkholder at the moment.

"I most certainly don't," Lucy retorted. Then, realizing how snobbish she must have sounded to Eve, she said, "I'm so chilled I can hardly feel my toes. But you two have *schpass*."

Without waiting for Nick's response, she entered the house with her stepsisters close on her heels. The mudroom was empty, but she could hear the clamor of guests in the kitchen. Her mind and stomach were spinning as she bent to unlace her boots.

"I *knew* you had an argument!" Mildred exclaimed, sounding far too happy for Lucy's liking. "He's trying to make you jealous, isn't he?"

As humiliated as she was by Nick's behavior, Lucy wasn't going to further embarrass herself by telling Mildred and Katura about their fake courtship. Covertly wiping her cheeks before she stood upright, Lucy replied, "*Neh.* He's showing hospitality to a visitor to Willow Creek, that's all."

"That's baloney," Katura stated emphatically. "Whatever you argued with him about, Lucy, you should just forget it or you're going to lose him."

"*Lose* him?" Lucy repeated incredulously. "He's not a coin! He's not a prize!"

"You know what I mean. He could court anyone he chooses," Katura said as she pulled off her gloves and stuffed them into the hood of her cloak before hanging it over someone else's coat on the crowded wall of pegs. "Although I don't see why he'd court a visitor like Eve when he hasn't even asked to be *my* suitor yet. But then, I didn't understand why he was pursuing you, either."

Lucy was so outraged she could hardly see straight

to open the door to the kitchen. Blindly she picked her way past the people milling about the snack table and clustered in the parlor. If there was one advantage to being so short it was that she could go unnoticed in times like these. Finally, securing the door of the vacant washroom, Lucy removed her glasses and leaned to splash water over her burning cheeks.

Straightening, she put her spectacles back on and peered into the mirror. She had to stand on her tiptoes to see the entirety of her facial reflection. Observing her mousy hair and unremarkable features, she knew she was no match for someone like Eve. The Amish didn't place an undue importance on physical appearances, but that didn't mean they had no sense of what was aesthetically pleasing. Lucy recognized there was nothing about her physical appearance *or* her personality that would have captured Nick's attention.

Why should I care? she asked herself. Their relationship wasn't real, so what did it matter if he was interested in Eve? *There is no* if. *He's definitely interested in her,* she thought. Or at least it appeared he was laying the groundwork for courting Eve. Nick no longer had a need for Lucy now that she had served her purpose. Here she thought she was one up on all the gullible young women—including her own cousin Bridget— who fawned over Nick and then were devastated when their courtships abruptly ended. Instead, Lucy was the most pathetic one of all, because their courtship was only pretend. But her hurt was very deep and very real.

She could hear singing in the next room. Lucy didn't want to join the others, but she couldn't ask Katura and Mildred to take her home already. She wasn't about to give them the satisfaction of knowing how much Nick had upset her. So, she contorted her mouth into a smile and joined the carolers, even though she didn't feel the least bit festive.

It took more time for Nick to untie Penny from the post and back the buggy out of the lane than it did for him to take Eve on a quick spin down the road and back. She chattered about the kinds of horses the *Englisch* brought to her father and some of the problems they encountered. Ordinarily, he would have been engrossed in the conversation, but his mind was preoccupied with Lucy. Nick was acutely aware of how bad it looked for him to take Eve for a ride while he was supposedly courting Lucy, and he hoped Lucy hadn't ended up telling her stepsisters their courtship was a sham. He couldn't wait to get back to speak to her alone.

He offered to drop Eve off at the door, but she said she'd keep him company while he hitched his horse to the post farther down the lane, closer to the stable. As they walked toward the house, she asked him something, but he was so antsy he didn't hear.

"What was that?" he asked when he realized she was waiting for a response.

"Melinda wasn't wrong. Sometimes I'm really off-key when I sing. But I didn't realize it was so noticeable to anyone else." Stalling on the porch, she added, "I really wish we didn't have to go back inside just yet."

"Well, if you want to stay outside, suit yourself, but I'm not going to hang out here," Nick said. The light from a nearby window illuminated Eve's crestfallen expression. He'd seen that look a dozen times. He hadn't meant to hurt her feelings, but he felt it was important to be up-front about where he stood; he had no romantic interest in Eve whatsoever. Still, he shouldn't have been so boorish. So she wouldn't feel personally rejected, in a softer tone Nick apologized, "I'm sorry, but I think Melinda may have given you the wrong idea about me. I'm… I'm kind of courting someone else."

"You are?" Eve's eyebrows shot up. "I didn't know. *Melinda* didn't know and she knows everything that goes on in Willow Creek… So, who is it you're courting?"

Nick feared she was doubting him, so he confessed, "It's Lucy Knepp, the woman I introduced you to. But listen, please don't mention it to anyone. Especially not to Melinda." If Lucy *had* already told her stepsisters the courtship was just an act after she saw Nick with Eve, Nick didn't want Melinda adding to the confusion by spreading rumors to the contrary.

"I won't," Eve promised. Nick wasn't sure whether he could trust her or not, but he was heartened by the fact she seemed to demonstrate more tact than her friend Melinda. She added, "Lucy must be pretty steamed with you right now. I know I would be if my suitor took another *maedel* for a ride."

"Hey, it wasn't my idea to go for a ride!" Nick protested.

"*Neh*, it wasn't. But that doesn't mean you're not to blame," Eve chastised him as they entered the mudroom. "You should have refused to go. That way you would have saved both me and Lucy from being upset about a misunderstanding."

Nick realized she was right and he promptly offered an apology for upsetting her, which Eve readily accepted. "I only hope Lucy is as forgiving as you are," he said.

But when he sidled up to Lucy on the periphery of the parlor, she pretended not to see him. She kept on singing even though he was so close he could have counted her individual eyelashes if they hadn't been so numerous.

"Lucy," he whispered during the chorus of a popular carol. "Can I talk to you in private?"

She stopped singing long enough to shush him from the corner of her mouth.

"There's something I need to tell you."

This time she turned toward him, scowling. In a hushed tone, she reprimanded, "Be quiet. We're trying to practice."

"But you're not even going to go caroling with them," he insisted.

Still glaring, she shook her head like a schoolteacher disappointed in a student, but she finally relented. The two of them backed out of the room and passed through the kitchen into the mudroom.

"Okay, so what is it you want to discuss?" she asked, wrapping her arms around her chest. It was cold enough for them to see their breath as they talked, and Nick shivered.

"Did you tell Katura and Mildred our courtship isn't real?"

"You dragged me out here to ask me *that*?" Lucy's voice was rising. Nick had some nerve. "If you were so worried about them finding out you're not really my suitor, you should have been a little more discreet about taking Eve for a ride in your buggy. That's not the behavior of a man who is genuinely courting a woman."

"But I asked you to *kumme* with us."

"Only because I caught you!" Lucy heard the screech in her own voice.

"You didn't *catch* me. I wasn't doing anything wrong."

Lucy inhaled deeply. Nick was right; technically, he wasn't doing anything wrong. What was the matter with her, acting as if he'd actually betrayed her by courting—or at least flirting with—another woman? Rationally, so as to diminish the intensity of her outburst, Lucy reasoned, "You know that and I know that, but Katura and Mildred don't know that. To them, it appeared you were seeing Eve behind my back or you were trying to make me jealous. Either way, I looked like a fool."

Nick's face was etched with lines. "I'm sorry I put you in an awkward position like that."

Since he really did look repentant, Lucy sighed and said, "It's okay, Nick. I denied there was any conflict between us, but I'll just tell Katura and Mildred you broke up with me and I didn't want to admit it."

Nick's big eyes drooped. "You're putting an end to our arrangement?"

"Well, I assume you don't need me now that you have Eve."

"I don't *have* Eve! I only took her for a ride because you weren't here and I wanted to get out of the house. Besides, it was the only way to get Melinda off my back. She was the one who practically pushed Eve into my buggy!"

Lucy felt more relieved than she cared to admit. Just to be sure she understood, she clarified, "So you still need me to cover for you while you make repairs to the cabin?"

"*Jah.* And despite my stupidity tonight, I hope you're still willing to."

Lucy sighed again. She wasn't quite sure she believed Nick had taken Eve for a ride just to appease Melinda. For all Lucy knew, Nick had proposed courtship and Eve had turned down his offer while they were out riding around. It was possible he was only coming back to Lucy because, once again, he had no other option. But then she reasoned if Nick wanted to continue their charade, it would still give her a chance to finish her project, which was the reason she'd agreed to the arrangement in the first place. Besides, she'd given Nick her word. She supposed she couldn't desert him now, for the sake of the Nelsons' Christmas reunion. But Lucy realized from now on she was going to have to keep her feelings in check. She couldn't afford to experience the kind of emotional turmoil she had tonight. It was too distressing, and she didn't want her Christmas season ruined.

"I'm still willing," she agreed. "But only until I finish *my* project. After that, we're 'breaking up,' whether or not you're done with the repairs." Then, just in case Nick still had any mistaken notion Lucy was a pushover, she added, "And when we do supposedly break up, we're going to say I'm the one who ended our courtship."

"All right," Nick said, nodding. *"Denki."*

He was so amenable to Lucy's conditions she almost wanted to rescind them. Almost, but not quite. *Don't let his big blue eyes or earnest expression get to you*, she reminded herself. *Or you'll end up like every other maedel he ever courted: sad and alone.*

Chapter Five

"I'm surprised Lucy's *eldre* allow her to go out so often," Nick's mother said to Nick before he went to milk the cows at first light on Monday morning. "I didn't mind you walking out with her on weeknights last week, but your *daed* has been looking especially run-down and I think he needs more rest. I'd like him to *kumme* home earlier in the evenings this week. You'll have to cut back on how much time you spend with Lucy so you can help Kevin at the store."

"All right, but I did promise I'd take her to the soup kitchen. The *Englisch* one where she serves supper on Wednesday nights. Is that okay?"

At the mention of the soup kitchen, Nick's mother said, "That's *wunderbaar* you're so committed to going to the soup kitchen with Lucy. Didn't I say she'd be a *gut* influence on you?"

Nick ambled to the barn, feeling guilty for allowing his mother to think he was actually going to help Lucy serve at the soup kitchen, when in fact he needed to reserve at least one evening away from the store during the week to work on the cabin. While he was milking the family's two cows, he reflected on the previous evening. Given how miffed Lucy had been about the business with Eve, Nick didn't look forward to calling off their previously arranged meeting tonight. While she said she forgave him, Lucy nevertheless had refused a ride from him, claiming she'd promised to wrangle her stepsisters home early that evening.

Not that he minded taking a break from being her pretend suitor. It was true that initially his fake courtship with Lucy had been more harmonious than any of his actual courtships, but their spat last night left him on shaky ground with her. That kind of conflict and sense of uneasiness inevitably resulted in Nick ending his relationships before things really soured or anyone's feelings were hurt even more. But this time, he didn't have the option of calling it quits, not until he completed the cabin repairs, anyway. *I'll have to keep things as amicable between us as possible for a couple more weeks*, he thought. Perhaps a brief separation would help toward that end.

Meanwhile, Nick was still at a loss on how to proceed with the repairs and he made it a priority to speak with Hunter and Fletcher that week. Since Hunter owned a furniture restoration shop on Main Street, Nick figured during a lunch break he could talk to him about replicating the color of the stain and the best method of application. As a carpenter, Fletcher frequented the hardware store, so Nick had hopes of speaking to him, too.

After breakfast Nick prepared to jot a note to Lucy informing her he had to cancel their evening plans. He'd give the written message to her sisters at the mercantile so they could deliver it to Lucy that afternoon.

He picked up a pen and stared at the blank sheet of paper, wondering how to word it. He would put the note in a sealed envelope, but that didn't guarantee her stepsisters wouldn't open it. He was probably wrong to suspect them of doing something like that, but he couldn't be too careful.

He hesitated with the pen angled an inch above the paper. Should he address her "dear Lucy?" Or just "Lucy"? He decided on just "Lucy," writing:

Lucy,
My father needs a break from the store a couple of evenings this week, so unfortunately I won't be able to follow through with our plans for tonight. But I'll see you Wednesday, when I'll pick you up to go to the soup kitchen.
Thank you for your understanding.

The note sounded dry to Nick so he added, "I look forward to being with you again," and hastily signed his name. It would have to do. As he sealed the envelope, a selfish thought crossed his mind: *Let's hope she isn't able to continue embroidering until then. I need her too much to allow her to end our courtship just yet.*

When Katura and Mildred returned home on Monday afternoon, Katura extended an envelope to Lucy. "It's from Nick."

"Denki." Lucy left the room so she could have some privacy, but her stepsisters followed her into the parlor. Betty was there, too, rocking in a chair and sipping tea. She greeted her daughters and asked what the commotion was about.

"Nick gave us a note for Lucy. Isn't that odd? We thought you were going out with him tonight. Couldn't he have waited until then to talk to you?"

It was frightfully cold outdoors and a draft swirled through the room so Lucy took a seat near the wood-stove. "Maybe something came up," she said, tearing the envelope open. After reading it, she announced, "See? I was right. Nick has to work at the store tonight because his *daed* is under the weather."

"Really?" Katura eyed her suspiciously.

Lucy thrust the letter at her. "Read it for yourself if you don't believe me." She was getting sick of her stepsisters doubting her word.

"Oh, I believe you. It's Nick I doubt. He was awfully friendly with Eve last night, no matter what excuse you claimed he gave you for taking her on a ride. Has it occurred to you he's getting ready to break off your courtship so he can court her instead?"

Lucy wanted to deny the possibility, but she wasn't positive she could defend Nick. She was still having the same doubts about him Katura had expressed.

"I doubt that's it," Betty interjected, to Lucy's surprise. "I was speaking to Nick's mother last week at church and she told me how worried she's been about her husband's health. Anyway, this works out better. Now Lucy can join us at Doris Plank's home this evening."

Every year Doris held a Christmas card–making event in her home. It was a time of celebration, and the Amish women from the Willow Creek district brought food for a potluck supper. Lucy generally loved the occasion, but she'd rather progress with her embroidery project.

"Actually, I have work to catch up on for my table-cloth for the auction," she said. "I'll stay behind and make supper for *Daed* and me."

"I've already prepared beef Stroganoff. There's enough for us to take and I've set aside some for him to have, too," Betty argued. "You really ought to *kumme*."

"I would, but I'm concerned about meeting the dead-line for the auc—"

"Lucy Knepp, sometimes I think you suffer from *hochmut*," Betty said, using the Amish word for pride. "If you would have had enough time to go out with Nick, you should have enough time to spend with the women from church. It's only one evening."

Lucy felt stung. *Hochmut?* That was the opposite of what she felt like most of the time. She didn't feel proud—she felt small. And not just physically small, either.

"All right," she agreed. Fighting tears, she rose and said, "I'm going to go finish my work in my room. I'll be down in time to go to the gathering at Doris's *haus*."

"As long as you're working tonight, I'm going to take off early," Kevin said to Nick after their father had left for the evening. "I haven't been out on a Mon-day in ages."

"It's hardly been a full week!" Nick exclaimed. "Be-sides, I'm not going to manage all the customers by myself."

"Why not? I handled the *Grischtdaag* shoppers with *Daed* all last week so you wouldn't have to."

Nick couldn't believe Kevin's unmitigated gall. "That's because I was out fixing *your* mess!"

"Really? How do I know you were working on the

cabin all that time? For all I know, you and Melinda's friend, Eve, spent most of last week walking out together while you were pretending to be working at the Nelsons' *haus*," Kevin suggested. "Don't deny it—I saw you leave with her last night. And I saw the look on Lucy's face when you came back in. You'll be fortunate if she doesn't blow your cover out of spite."

"You're really something, you know that, Kevin? You've got to stop gossiping—it's going to get you in a lot of trouble some day. Especially since you don't have a clue about what's going on."

"I know a scorned *maedel* when I see one. I'm beginning to think little Lucy Knepp has a crush on you. Are you sure she knows this phony arrangement is temporary?"

"*Jah*, but it's going to be a lot more temporary if you don't knock it off, because I'll quit working on Jenny's cabin in a heartbeat if you so much as think about abandoning your duties here this evening."

"All right, no need to get huffy," Kevin griped.

Despite his bluster, Nick was concerned. How many others had noticed he'd left the singing with Eve? His father's health was precarious—Nick couldn't let anything jeopardize the secrecy about the fire Kevin had started. He was beginning to wonder if he should have let Kevin suffer the consequences of his actions. But then, that would have meant their father would suffer, too. Nick had come this far; he couldn't allow that to happen now.

But how could he be sure Lucy was still as dedicated to protecting their shared secret as Nick was? After all, this was the same woman who'd been a notorious snitch when she was a child. But that was ages ago and

Nick couldn't imagine Lucy exposing their secret, especially not out of spite. In order for her to be spiteful, she would have had to be romantically interested in Nick in the first place. And if he'd ever thought that was possible, their interaction the previous evening rid his mind utterly of such a notion.

Nick resigned himself to putting his worries aside and focusing on the steady stream of customers winding their way through the store's aisles. As it happened, Fletcher Chupp was among them so Nick was able to ask his questions about the drywall for his project.

After advising him, Fletcher remarked, "Sounds like you're doing some hefty renovating. I don't remember there being paneling in your *haus*."

Nick coughed, stalling. "*Neh*, there isn't. This is for a…a part-time job I've taken on after hours. Just don't mention it to anyone, all right? It's a long story, but it's sort of a *Grischtdaag* surprise."

"Mum's the word," Fletcher said. "I've been staying late on my job, too—so I can build a new chest of drawers for my wife. Although I wouldn't be surprised if she knows already. Women are intuitive like that. Nothing gets past them."

Thinking of Lucy's stepsisters and of Melinda Schrock, plus his own mother, Nick could only hope that wasn't true.

There were at least two dozen women at Doris Plank's house and Lucy was glad she went. After sharing their potluck entrées, the women got busy making cards. Sending and receiving homemade Christmas cards was a cherished Amish tradition in Willow Creek, and designing them was one of Lucy's favorite activities because it increased her anticipation of the upcoming holiday and allowed her to keep in touch with people she held dear.

"Look at that, you're so creative," Doris commented over Lucy's shoulder as she circled the tables serving cookies. Lucy had used construction paper, glue and a sprinkle of glitter to create two pairs of skates hanging side by side from hooks. Next to them was a window with a wreath in it, and snow was falling outside the panes. The card was for Bridget.

"Denki," Lucy said without looking up. "But I don't think it's really very creative. It's more like a habit. When you embroider as much scenery as I do for the *Englisch*, it becomes second nature."

"Jah, Betty told me you were decorating a beautiful tablecloth for the Piney Hill festival. And Melinda Schrock said you've been a busy beaver, filling specialty orders for customers at the shop. How do you do it all?"

Lucy was amazed such mundane details of her life were fodder for Melinda and Doris's conversations. "It's not so difficult," she said. "I get a lot done in the evenings when I—"

Too late she realized she was on the brink of giving her secret away. Not knowing how to explain, she bit into a cookie and then tried to change the subject, saying through a full mouth, "These are *appenditlich*. Did you make them, Doris?"

"Don't let Lucy fool you," Betty cut in. "She hasn't been working as much as she says. She's been going out with a certain suitor nearly every evening. If he hadn't been busy, she wouldn't be here tonight."

Lucy wanted to slink beneath the table. The worst

part of Betty's gossiping was that she was beaming, as if being courted by Nick Burkholder was Lucy's greatest achievement in life.

"A certain suitor?" Doris's ears seemed fine-tuned to the slightest mention of a courtship. "I had no idea you were walking out with someone. But if I had to venture a guess, I'd say it's Frederick Stutzman. Am I right?"

Lucy dabbed a cotton swab into a pool of glue and then applied it to her card. How could it be Doris had heard the minutest details of Lucy's life, yet didn't know Lucy had turned down Frederick's offer of courtship? Speechless, she shook her head in reply to Doris's question.

"If we guess, will you tell us?" Melinda Schrock taunted from the far end of the table where she was seated next to Eve.

"Oh, leave her alone," Eve scolded, to Lucy's surprise. "In my district in Ohio we don't talk about our courtships."

Iris Schwartz chimed in, "We don't usually discuss them publicly in Willow Creek, and we don't pressure others into discussing them, either. Doris, please pass that cookie platter this way."

Lucy appreciated their tactful scolding, but Doris and Melinda ignored their hints to drop the subject.

"That's okay, I already know who it is," Melinda said in a singsong voice. "It's someone named Dan Ebersole, isn't it? I've heard about a young man who's new to the area and he volunteers at the soup kitchen where Lucy serves. It's got to be him. There's no one else who's available."

Lucy was mortified. All she needed was for Melinda to start a rumor that Dan was Lucy's suitor. She liked him as a friend, of course, but as his friend Lucy didn't want Dan to think Lucy had started the rumor. For a split second, she considered telling everyone at the table it was Nick, not Dan, who was her suitor. Somewhat surprised Betty didn't volunteer that information herself, Lucy glanced at her stepmother, who caught her eye and winked at her.

"There's no one else available to do what?" Mildred asked as she pranced into the room carrying another tray of cookies.

"To court Lucy. She's got her first suitor and she won't tell us who it is," Doris announced. Lucy was mortified she emphasized the fact this was Lucy's first suitor—especially because he wasn't actually her suitor at all. Did all of the women in Willow Creek know she'd never been courted?

"Oh, that's easy," Mildred said, and Lucy wished she could reach across the room and clap her hand over Mildred's mouth. "It's Nick Burkholder."

"Ha!" Melinda sneered. "If he turned down the chance to court Eve, he wouldn't court Lucy."

"Melinda!" Eve exclaimed. "What kind of thing is that to say? He probably has no interest in me *because* he's courting Lucy."

Lucy didn't know what was more humiliating: Melinda's proclamation Lucy was less desirable for courtship than Eve was, or Eve's condescending denial. She wanted to flee the room, but the heaviness in her stomach kept her anchored to her chair.

Eve's admonishment, coupled with the other women's silence, must have shamed Melinda into recognizing how offensive her remark was. "I didn't mean it the way it came out. I just meant Nick is so outgoing and so is Eve, and Lucy, well, you're as quiet as a church mouse."

Lucy wanted to tell Melinda what animal *she* was as loud as, but instead she silently prayed for grace.

"Sometimes opposites attract," Betty stated. Her face was blotchy, as if she were the one who'd been insulted, not Lucy.

"That's very true. In some ways, John and I are as different as night and day. For example, he used to love *kaffi* but I only liked tea," Doris said. "Yet while we were courting, he drank tea just to please me. It was so romantic."

As Doris continued to blather on about trivial differences between her and her husband, Lucy fought back tears. She wished she could sneak away to the washroom, but if she did, she'd draw more attention to how uncomfortable she felt. So she continued to work on her card for Bridget. *I'll be so glad when she gets here*, she thought. Bridget would understand how Lucy felt.

Knowing that Betty, Katura and Mildred wouldn't leave the party until everyone else did, Lucy tried to make the most of the evening. After finishing her cards, she went into the kitchen for a glass of water. She was turning from the sink when Eve walked in. Lucy briefly nodded and started toward the hall, but Eve stopped her.

"Lucy, I'm so sorry I let it slip that Nick's your suitor," she said quietly. "I didn't mean to, but I was so appalled at Melinda's remarks it just came out."

"It's all right," Lucy replied. "Mildred was the one who told everyone first."

"Well, for the record, I honestly wasn't all that interested in being courted by Nick. I mean, I *am* interested in having a suitor and Nick seems like a nice person. But I mainly went for a ride with him to keep Melinda from embarrassing both of us even more than she'd already done by pushing us together."

Lucy eyed Eve skeptically. Was she telling the truth?

"Melinda is my best friend from childhood and I love her dearly. She grew up without a *mamm* or any female influences in her life when she was a young *maedel*, so she lacks some of the…the sensitivity or *gut* manners other *meed* have. But sometimes I can't believe she hasn't matured more," Eve explained. Then she added, "Just so you know, Nick wasn't happy about taking me for a ride, either. He was so concerned about what you'd think he couldn't wait to get back."

Even though Lucy knew the reason Nick couldn't wait to get back was because he wanted to be sure she hadn't told her stepsisters they weren't actually courting, she was glad to hear he wasn't really interested in Eve. Lucy regretted not taking him at his word when he made the same claim himself.

Eve chewed on her lip before continuing, "I understand why you'd be upset with me, but please don't be upset with Nick. It's not my place to say, but he really cares about you. I knew it from the look in his eyes when he saw you near the porch and invited you to *kumme* with us. I should have told him right then and there I didn't want to go for a ride. I should have stepped aside and let you go with him alone. But I selfishly didn't want to face Melinda's interrogation if I returned to the *haus* without Nick, and I'm sorry about that."

Eve could tell Nick cared about Lucy? Nick might have cared about her as a friend, and he definitely cared about preserving their arrangement, but it was a bit of a stretch for Lucy to believe he cared about her romantically, the way Eve was implying. "*Denki* for telling me all of that. But there's no need to apologize. I assure you, nothing you did affected my...my relationship with Nick."

Eve clasped her hands together against her chest. "That's *wunderbaar* to hear because he seemed very worried about it. Not that I blame him—you're so talented and pretty. It probably took a lot for him to ask to court you in the first place. Men can be insecure like that sometimes. At least, that's why I tell myself I've only ever had one suitor."

Lucy was surprised by Eve's compliment, which seemed genuine even though she'd never before been called *pretty* by anyone other than her father, as well as by Eve's admission she'd only had one suitor. Lucy would have thought someone as gregarious and becoming as Eve would have had men lining up to court her—to marry her, in fact.

Lucy touched Eve's arm. "Those men in Ohio can't be too smart to pass you by," she said. But inwardly, Lucy was glad the men in Willow Creek—and Nick, in particular—had passed Eve by, too.

Nick rubbed his hands against his legs as he headed to Lucy's house on Wednesday night. As frigid as the air was, his palms were sweaty from the apprehension of seeing her again. But when she approached his buggy, she was all smiles. He eagerly offered assistance into the carriage, which she accepted since she was carrying a big plastic container she indicated held Christmas cookies.

"I, uh…it's really cold. You might need this," he stuttered, unfolding yet another blanket to add to the two she was already securing around her lap. As he bent down to arrange it around her feet, he clunked his head against hers and dropped back against the seat.

"Ouch!" he exclaimed. "Sorry, sorry. Are you okay?"

Lucy laughed, rubbing her head. "Fortunately, I think my bonnet absorbed the force of the blow."

He was glad she was so forgiving, but once again his size and ungainliness made him feel like an ox around her, both physically and verbally. Lucy, on the other hand, was extraordinarily chatty that evening. All the way there, she talked about how much she loved the month of December at the soup kitchen. She said during the holiday season several local *Englisch* companies donated an abundance of delicious treats and items such as toys, toothbrushes and wool socks for the people who came there to eat.

"I wish I could knit. Then I could make socks, too," she lamented.

"You don't knit? But you're embroidering an entire tablecloth," he said.

She giggled. "Knitting and embroidery are nothing alike. Sadly, I can't knit or crochet. I ought to make a resolution to learn because they're both much more useful skills than embroidering is."

"But your linens bring in an income. And you're using your talent to raise funds for the soup kitchen. How can you say embroidery isn't useful?" Nick marveled.

Lucy cocked her head thoughtfully. "I suppose it is. It's just… I don't know. Haven't you ever wished you had a skill that you don't have?"

Nick nodded. "*Jah*. I wish I could sing better," he admitted. "My voice is *baremlich*. Sometimes during church worship, I mouth the words. I'm thinking about what they mean and I'm trying to praise the Lord in thought, but I'm not singing aloud. I wouldn't inflict noise like that on everyone else."

Even though he was serious, Lucy laughed. "*Kumme* now, it can't be that bad. Besides, you're singing to the Lord. What business is it of anyone else's how *Gott* made your voice to sound?"

She was right, and Nick momentarily regretted having shared this shortcoming with her, knowing it made him seem vain. But then Lucy added, "For what it's worth, I think your speaking voice is pleasant. It's very masculine and comforting. Not too loud or overbearing, the way some men's voices can be."

Nick was sure he was blushing. "*Denki,*" he replied, relieved his voice didn't crack when he said it.

As they pulled up to the parking lot in front of the church where the soup kitchen was located, Nick spotted a young man on the sidewalk beneath the lights. Lucy simultaneously yanked the blankets over her head and dropped to her hands and knees on the floor of the buggy, causing Nick to halt the carriage.

"What's wrong?" he asked.

"That's Dan Ebersole. Usually my *daed* brings me here. Dan can't see me arriving with you. He'll think we're actually courting."

Nick was confused. He lifted the blankets enough to peek at Lucy and asked, "Isn't that what we want people to think?"

Peeping up at him, Lucy said, "*Jah*, I guess you're right." Then she stood and brushed off her skirt. "Sorry.

I've heard a lot of…of far-fetched gossip lately, and I suppose I panicked when I saw one of my peers. But since you and I will be ending our arrangement in a couple weeks anyway, I'd prefer that as few people as possible know we're supposedly courting. Too many already know about it, which means they'll all find out when we 'break up,' too. It's going to be awkward enough as it is to be the subject of that kind of gossip among our peers. The soup kitchen is the one public place I go where none of my peers go. Except for Dan, I mean. So I'd prefer it if he didn't find out about either our courtship or our breakup, if that makes sense. So would you mind dropping me off here? And can you pick me up a little later, say eight fifteen, so no one sees you?"

Nick agreed, "Of course. Hold on a minute and I'll help you down."

But Lucy insisted she could manage, and she was out of the buggy and down the walkway in a flash. Nick watched as she caught up with Dan, who turned and grinned and then carried the container of cookies for her.

At the cabin while he used the technique Hunter advised to apply stain to the new pieces of paneling, Nick thought about Lucy's reaction to seeing Dan. Rather, to Dan possibly seeing her. Her explanation about why she wanted to limit the number of people who knew about their pretend courtship made sense, but Nick couldn't help but wonder if Lucy was interested in being courted by Dan. Maybe that was really why she didn't want Dan to see her with him. The thought shouldn't have bothered Nick, but he was so distracted he spilled stain on the floor and then spent the remaining time cleaning it up.

Afterward he was relieved that when he picked up Lucy Dan was nowhere in sight.

"Was your evening productive?" Lucy asked as they got underway.

"Actually, I spent more time fixing my own mess than I did cleaning up Kevin's," Nick said.

"Kevin was helping you?" Lucy asked, startling Nick. He hadn't intended to mention his brother. His mind was really not where it should be tonight.

"*Neh.* But he borrowed my tool kit and I couldn't find anything I was looking for in it. Kevin's not the most organized person in the world." It wasn't a lie— Kevin *had* borrowed his tool kit and returned it in disarray, but that wasn't the mess Nick had been referring to.

Lucy clicked her tongue sympathetically. "That sounds like what Mildred does when she borrows something from my sewing basket."

Relieved, Nick asked, "How was your evening?"

"It was *wunderbaar.* Because of the cold weather, we had twice as many people *kumme* in as usual, so the place was jammed. Since the oven's broken, we couldn't prepare warm meals, but we put on a spread of picnic foods like potato salad and burgers and hot dogs, which the men made on the grills everyone brought."

"Ah, I get it. Instead of a '*Grischtdaag* in July' event, you had a 'July at *Grischtdaag*' supper."

Lucy clapped her gloved hands. "Oh, very clever! We should have thought to call it that."

Nick grinned, pleased she found his idea clever.

Lucy was chipper as she described the scene at the soup kitchen, and her mirth buoyed Nick's mood, as well.

"There was a high school choir there singing *Grischtdaag* songs while everyone ate, and afterward we got to distribute some of the donated items. That was the best part. I don't know why *Gott* allows me to be in a position to witness joy like that, but I'm so grateful He does."

Moved by her sentiment, Nick stole a sideways glance at Lucy. She was glowing, her face directed toward the sky. He felt like he was the one who got to witness pure joy.

"Look!" she suddenly demanded. "Is that snow?"

Sure enough, white flakes dotted the night sky. They were so light they floated instead of fell, but they were undeniably snowflakes.

"I do believe it is," he replied.

"It's snowing!" Lucy yelled, pushing the blankets aside. She stood and flung her arms in the air. "It's snowing!"

"Hey, you're going to fall," Nick cautioned, attempting to slow the horse at the same time he reached to steady Lucy.

"*Neh*, I'm not. Don't slow down, please," she pleaded. "Go faster. Faster!"

"You're *narrish*!" he declared, but he honored her request to increase their speed, keeping one hand against the small of her back in support.

She rode like that for a good two miles, her arms outstretched, her face tipped toward the sky. Her outer winter bonnet slipped from her head and dangled by its ribbons down her back. She removed her glasses, saying they were too wet to see through, and that's when

Nick noticed what a gentle profile she had, with her delicately pointed nose and sharp cheekbones.

Finally, as they approached the bend toward her house, he said, "I think you should sit down now, Lucy. I don't want you to fall when we round the next corner."

"All right," she agreed readily, dropping to the seat. She was so close to him that if he had moved his knee an inch, it would have touched hers, but surprisingly she made no attempt to move away. Beneath a streetlamp, Nick could see her cheeks glistened with snow and the bun in her hair was coming loose.

"We, ah, better stop here so you can pull yourself together," he suggested.

"Ach, do I look that bad?" Lucy asked, although she giggled as if she hardly cared.

Actually, she didn't look bad at all. She looked, well, she looked *free*. She looked the way Nick felt whenever Penny ran this fast—as if everything was exciting and anything was possible. "*Neh*, but your hair is coming down, here," Nick said, gently lifting a strand. His hand trembled. "And I don't know where your prayer *kapp* is, but your bonnet is hanging down your back. I wouldn't want anyone to think…"

Modesty kept him from saying what he feared others might think, but Lucy seemed to catch on right away. "*Neh*, of course not," she said. When she lifted her hand to fix her hair, it bumped his hand, which made him realize he was still holding the silky lock between his fingers.

After fixing her bun and looking around in vain for her prayer *kapp*, Lucy donned her bonnet and tied it beneath her chin. They continued in silence to her house, where Nick bounced down to help her from the carriage, extending his hand. Her small fingers disappeared within his larger ones, but instead of stepping down, she lingered there until his eyes met hers.

"*Denki*, Nick. That was exhilarating."

Exhilarated was exactly what Nick felt when he looked at Lucy. He swallowed and said, "Anytime."

Chapter Six

Lucy was so jubilant after her Wednesday night buggy ride with Nick she didn't even object when Betty said she ought to accompany her, Katura and Mildred on a trip to visit their relatives in Elmsville for supper on Thursday evening. Although she was slightly behind where she wanted to be with her special embroidery project, Lucy figured on Friday night she and Nick would be able to stay out later so she could catch up then.

On Friday morning, she journeyed into town with her stepsisters to drop off an order at Schrock's Shop. Joseph Schrock, who managed the family-run business, was delighted to see her.

"Your linens are flying off the shelf, Lucy," he said. "One customer wanted to buy all of your Christmas place mats. I limited her to a set of six because I didn't want to disappoint other customers, but I promised I'd ask if you could make an extra twelve for them by next Thursday, the fifteenth. They're having a special family gathering this *Grischtdaag* and they want enough place mats for eighteen people. If you're not able to make them by then, they'd like to know so they'll have time to *kumme* up with something else to adorn their table."

Lucy hesitated. The place mats' intricate poinsettia pattern was more time-consuming than some of her simpler designs. She wasn't sure she could fulfill that request, plus keep up with her other orders and finish the tablecloth for the auction, as well. "I hesitate to commit to that," she said. "My hands are full with other things I need to do before *Grischtdaag*."

Lucy was unaware Melinda had sidled up to her until she butted in. "It's probably difficult to keep up with work when you've got so many...shall we say, *social commitments*." Because Melinda was married to Joseph's nephew, Jesse, she worked at the shop, and Lucy silently asked the Lord to prevent her from saying anything more about her courtship with Nick. It was bad enough most of the women in Willow Creek knew; Lucy didn't want the men knowing, too. It would only make things more awkward when her arrangement with Nick ended.

"Social commitments?" Joseph repeated blankly.

Concerned Melinda was about to go into detail, Lucy quickly offered, "I'll do my best to embroider another twelve place mats by Thursday, Joseph. I'll deliver them that afternoon, sometime after four o'clock."

He grinned. "*Denki*, Lucy. I knew you weren't the type to put pleasure before work."

Joseph shot a pointed look at Melinda.

Lucy understood he intended his remark as a compliment, but it rubbed her the wrong way. Didn't people think she liked to have any fun at all? After paying

Lucy, Joseph walked away quickly to serve a customer in the candle and soaps aisle.

Apparently, Melinda was supposed to be working the cash register, and she sauntered to the other side of the checkout counter and said, "I heard Wheeler's Pond is frozen over. If this cold snap keeps up, some of us are going skating tomorrow night. You and Nick should *kumme*. Unless you're too busy sewing. Or unless he can't make it for some reason."

Lucy felt more like Melinda was challenging her than inviting her to join their peers for skating. It was as if Melinda doubted Lucy and Nick were a couple. They weren't, of course, but Lucy was provoked all the same. "I'd really like that," she said. "I'm going to the hardware store next, so I'll see what Nick thinks of the idea. Usually he likes to keep me all to himself, but maybe tomorrow evening we'll squeeze in a little social time with the rest of you."

When Melinda's lower lip jutted out in a pout, Lucy felt victorious. But, after exiting the shop, she paused on the front stoop and clasped her hands together to keep them from shaking. It was true she'd intended to go to the hardware store next, but not to talk to Nick. Not specifically, anyway. She planned to purchase a toolbox for her father's wood-carving tools for Christmas. Now how was she going to break it to Nick she'd just committed them to showing up for skating on Saturday evening? Lucy considered not telling him at all, but she couldn't put it past Melinda to check up on her by questioning Nick. He deserved fair warning.

Lucy was only halfway through the entrance when she spotted Nick chatting with an *Englisch* customer, who held his rapt attention. Noticing the way Nick's strong hands gestured as he spoke, Lucy was reminded of how safe she had felt when he'd steadied her in the buggy the other night. A shiver wiggled down her spine, just as it had done from his touch that night. She heard Nick wish the customer success with his renovation, and then he turned in Lucy's direction. A wide smile broke across his freckled cheeks.

"Hi, Lucy," he said, ambling in her direction. "How are you today?"

"I'm fine, *denki*. I'm here to purchase a case or a toolbox. For wood-carving tools. Chisels. Knives. That kind of thing." Lucy was so nervous she could hardly communicate, but Nick didn't seem to notice.

"So you've taken up wood carving in addition to embroidery?" he joked.

"*Neh*, it's not for me. It's a present for my *daed* for *Grischtdaag*. But if you see him, don't tell him," she replied solemnly.

"I can keep a secret," Nick promised, winking at her. Her knees went weak then, and again when he touched the small of her back and ushered her down an aisle. "We keep our toolboxes over here. What kind are you looking for?"

"The best kind," she said, flustered by his nearness.

Nick threw his head back and laughed. "Well, that's *gut* because we don't stock the worst kind." His laughter put Lucy at ease and she chuckled, too. Then he questioned whether she wanted a wood or plastic toolbox.

"I guess I don't know what I'm looking for."

As Nick began to show Lucy the different types of boxes, she had a difficult time focusing on his descriptions. She felt heady from watching his hands pulling open the little drawers, from his masculine, musky scent, and from the clean, smooth skin of his jaw. She had to tell him about the skating at Wheeler's Pond now, before she lost her nerve.

"So, what do you think?" He paused, waiting for her response.

"I'll take whatever you recommend," she said. "I trust your advice."

Nick smiled and removed the wooden box from the shelf. "Then you'll definitely want this one. It's a little more expensive, but the feature that allows you to tilt the knife compartment for easier access is worth it," he said, and began to walk down the aisle, but Lucy grabbed him by the crook of his arm.

"I told Melinda we'd go skating at Wheeler's Pond tomorrow night." Her words were both quiet and rushed.

"You what?" Nick asked, leaning closer. He smelled so good. Too good. She released his arm.

"I told Melinda we'd go skating at Wheeler's Pond on Saturday," Lucy repeated. "I'm sorry. She was badgering me and I just—well, I don't know what came over me. We can make up an excuse not to go, but I had to tell you now so we can get our story straight in case she pops in here and interrogates you about it."

She held her breath, waiting for his response.

Nick couldn't take his eyes off Lucy. The color rising to her cheeks reminded him of how she had looked on Wednesday night after her madcap performance in his buggy. He wanted to say he'd love to go skating with her, but he wasn't sure she actually wanted to go to the pond herself. She was only telling him so they could come up with an excuse not to go, right? Nick didn't feel confident enough to ask her outright.

"I suppose after I'm done working on the cabin and if you're satisfied with your progress embroidering, we could stop by the pond," he suggested. "For the sake of appearances, that is."

Lucy let her breath out. "Are you sure you don't mind?"

"*Neh*, not at all. I enjoy skating. Haven't done it in years but I wouldn't mind taking a spin around the rink."

"Oh, Nick, that's *wunderbaar*," Lucy whispered. "For appearances, I mean."

Nick felt deflated. He shifted the large toolbox in his arms and asked, "So do you really need one of these, or was that just a pretense to *kumme* talk to me in private?"

"I really need one," she said in a normal voice again.

He led her back to the cash register, where Kevin had taken over ringing up the sales. "Lucy gets the carpenter's discount," Nick told his brother.

"Oh, she's building a *haus*, is she?" Kevin asked her.

Nick glared at his brother. Before turning his attention to another customer, Nick said, "If it's okay with you, I'll pick you up half an hour earlier tonight, Lucy. Kevin likes to assist the customers without my help. It makes him feel like he's in charge."

Kevin opened his mouth, and then closed it and grunted.

"I'll look forward to that, Nick," Lucy said sweetly. If she was surprised Nick was being so obvious about their supposed courtship in front of Kevin, she didn't let on.

The rest of the morning flew by, and soon Nick's mother stopped in with lunch for the four of them to eat in the back room. Nick noticed his father picking at his food; ordinarily, he had a hearty appetite. "We've got things covered at the shop today, *Daed*," he said. "You could go home with *Mamm* after lunch if you want."

Kevin still must have been peeved about Nick's earlier remark because he said, "*Jah*, Nick is so confident in my abilities, he's leaving half an hour early to take Lucy out tonight."

If Kevin was hoping to get Nick in hot water, his plan backfired. "I'm confident in your abilities to handle the store alone, too, Kevin, so I think I will go home after lunch," their father said. Then he turned to Nick. "Lucy's a *wunderbaar maedel*. You can leave even earlier if you'd like to."

"*Denki*, but that's not necessary," Nick said. Then, taking advantage of the opportunity, he added, "But I would like to get out of work a little earlier tomorrow afternoon so I can spend more time with her. She, uh, has some special things I'm helping her accomplish before *Grischtdaag*, and then in the evening we're going skating on Wheeler's Pond."

"Is Lucy up for that?" his mother asked. "She's in such frail health."

The potato he'd been chewing felt like it was lodged in Nick's throat. He coughed and thumped his fist against his chest. "What do you mean, she's in frail health?"

His mother swallowed before she answered. "Lucy's prone to pneumonia. Last year she had such a bad case of it she wound up hospitalized for nearly a week. It's a result of being born so early and having all those respiratory problems. You'd better be sure she stays bundled up, *suh*. Skating might be fine for half an hour or so, but don't overdo it."

Nick shook his head in disbelief. He never knew Lucy suffered from any kind of illness. After watching her stunt in the buggy on Wednesday night, he thought she was one of the toughest girls he'd ever courted. Why had she agreed to go skating if she was prone to pneumonia? "I didn't know she was in poor health. She never told me," he admitted.

"Ach!" his mother patted her lips with a napkin. "Listen to me. What a tale-teller I am. She probably didn't mention it because it's been such a struggle for her, but her *daed* says she prefers to keep it to herself and to act as if she's fine. He worries about her, though. So don't you give him extra cause for concern."

"I won't, *Mamm*," Nick promised.

For the rest of the afternoon he experienced a growing mix of concern and anger. He didn't want Lucy to get sick, yet he resented it that she'd put him in a position of jeopardizing her health. That wasn't fair. There was no way he was going skating with her now, no matter what Melinda deduced from their absence.

Later, when Lucy climbed into the buggy Nick placed a fourth blanket on her lap before signaling Penny to walk on.

"What's this for?" she asked. "I can barely move."

"You didn't tell me you were sick," he said accusingly. "That wasn't fair."

"What are you talking about? I'm not sick."

He pulled the buggy off the road. "You're prone to pneumonia," he accused.

Lucy stiffened. "I see some *bobblemoul* has been filling your ears with gossip."

Bristling to hear Lucy unwittingly refer to his mother as a blabbermouth, Nick replied, "It's not gossip if it's true."

"*Neh*, it's not slander if it's true, but it's still gossip," Lucy argued. "Either way, I don't see how it's any of your business."

"None of my business? I wouldn't have taken you out in this frigid weather if I had known about your health condition. You should have told me rather than to put me in this position."

Lucy slapped her hands against her lap. "I'm an adult. I don't need to get permission from you to go outside during the winter."

"Maybe not, but did you ever think what would have happened if you'd gotten pneumonia?"

"*Jah*, I would have suffered from it. Me. Not you. I would've been the one in the hospital."

Nick raised his voice. "Don't act like that, Lucy. Don't deny it wouldn't have had an effect on me, too. I would have known I was responsible."

"What are you talking about? You're not responsible for me. *I'm* responsible for me. And so is the Lord. I don't understand why you're being like this all of a sudden. If you want to put an end to our arrangement for some other reason, just tell me. You don't need to create some pitiful excuse."

Nick was so frustrated he took off his hat and smacked it against his fist. "I'm not creating an excuse. Your health is a perfectly valid reason to call off our deal. I don't see why you can't understand that."

"Okay," Lucy said, moving toward the edge of the

seat. "Deal's off." She jumped down before Nick could stop her and began walking in the direction of her house.

"Lucy! *Kumme* back here," he called. "You're being *lecherich*!"

Lucy turned and shouted, "I'm not your responsibility anymore, Nick. Not that I ever was. So leave me alone."

If Nick wasn't mistaken, she was crying. In all of the times he'd broken off a relationship, he had never felt as miserable as he did now when making Lucy Knepp cry. And his courtship with her wasn't even real. He couldn't let it end like this. Within a few paces, he'd caught up to her and a few paces after that, he'd gained enough ground to turn around and face her as she approached, holding his arms out to prevent her passage.

"Knock it off, Nick," Lucy shouted, tears streaming down her face. "I want to get by."

"And I want to take you home. *Kumme* on, Lucy. Be reasonable."

Even in her outrage, Lucy could see the sense in what he was saying. For one thing, it was bitterly cold. For another, if her father found out she'd walked home in that kind of weather, he'd be furious—not at Lucy, but at Nick. That wouldn't be fair.

"Fine." She turned and headed back toward the buggy. When he offered his hand, she pushed it away.

Nick took his seat next to her and picked up the reins, but before moving onward, he said, "I don't understand it, Lucy. Why is my caring about you such an awful thing?" His voice was quivering and Lucy felt a pang of guilt. She knew she was overreacting. Rather, she was reacting to a heartache that had plagued her for years, not one Nick had caused that evening.

"I don't expect you to understand," she said, wiping her rough woolen mitten across her cheeks.

"But I want to. Can't you explain it to me?"

Nick's voice was so forlorn Lucy let her defenses drop. "I've always been treated like this, my entire life. *Lucy's too weak, too fragile, too small, she can't go outside or run around or have any fun because she'll get sick. She'll stop breathing. She'll wind up in the hospital.* My whole life, Nick. And then, the one little taste of utter abandon I ever experienced—charging through the dark with a frosty wind whisking against my face, feeling totally invigorated and alive—you want to take that away from me, too."

She was crying so hard her words were barely intelligible, but Nick didn't interrupt or attempt to quiet her. When she finally settled down and could speak normally again, she sniffed and asked, "May I use your handkerchief, please?"

"Sorry, I don't have one," Nick said. "But here, you can use my scarf. I don't mind."

The offer to use Nick's scarf to dry her eyes and blow her nose was so ridiculous and sweet all at once it caused Lucy to chuckle. "*Neh*, that's okay," she said, removing her mittens to dab her eyes with her bare fingers.

"I really am sorry," he repeated.

Lucy was embarrassed. "That's all right. I've stopped blubbering. I don't need a handkerchief after all."

"*Neh*, I mean I'm sorry I treated you in a way that made you feel…the way you feel. I didn't mean to. I was concerned. I care about you and I wouldn't want anything to happen to you. I especially wouldn't want to play a role in hurting you."

Lucy was overwhelmed by his words. No man had ever said anything like that to her before, even in friendship. "It's not your fault," she said. "And I do appreciate that you care. But I'm not as fragile as you think I am."

"Fragile? You? I don't think you're fragile at all, even if you are prone to pneumonia," Nick scoffed. "I think you're one of the most resilient women I've ever known."

Lucy was overwhelmed again. If this kept up, she was going to fall hard for Nick Burkholder. Maybe she already had. "Then let's continue our arrangement. We both have work left to do."

"Okay, but you have to promise me something," Nick said, peering at her. In the dark she could only make out the whites of his eyes but his voice was heavy. "Promise you'll tell me if all this running around gets to be too much for you. And if you even think there's a chance you're catching a cold, you have to—"

"I'll tell you," Lucy promised somberly. Then, in a lighter tone she said, "So in that vein, I'm getting cold now. Can we keep going, please?"

Nick released the buggy's parking brake and clicked for Penny to move on. They'd traveled a few hundred yards when he shook his head. It seemed he was thinking aloud as he said, "So when we were *kinner* in school…all those times you stayed inside and cleaned the whiteboards… That was because you weren't allowed to go outside?"

"That's right," Lucy said with a sigh. "I used to watch the rest of you from the window and daydream about what it would be like to be out there running around or playing hide-and-seek."

"No wonder you were always tattling on us. You must have been pretty envious."

Lucy was indignant. "I never tattled on anyone!" she said. "Not once, ever. Especially not on you. I loved watching your antics even if—sometimes *especially if*—you misbehaved. If I'd told on you, the teacher would have made you quit climbing trees or hiding lunch boxes or whatever other mischief you were causing. I would have been bored out of my skull just watching the girls playing jacks."

"Really?" Nick asked, and Lucy vehemently assured him she was telling the truth.

"I didn't even tell when you nicknamed me Bug Eyes."

"Did I do that?" Nick asked. "I honestly don't remember."

"Well, I sure do."

"Wow, I'm sorry. No wonder my nickname was Naughty Nick."

Lucy giggled. "I'd rather be known as Naughty Nick than Lovely Lucy. That was a hard title to live up to. But it was better than Bug Eyes." She affectionately nudged Nick's arm with hers.

He shook his head again. "Like I said, I honestly don't remember doing that. But in my defense, I really did love insects. So Bug Eyes might have been a compliment."

"*Jah*, nice try!" Lucy laughed. "It doesn't matter. I forgave you long ago. I wasn't really so lovely myself, and I had a lot of things I needed to be forgiven for, too. I still do."

Nick turned slightly in his seat. "For what it's worth, I'd never call you Bug Eyes now. Your eyes are beautiful, like a doe's," he said. Then he worried aloud, "That isn't an offensive wildlife association is it?"

"Not at all," Lucy murmured. It was lovely. Who would have thought it would take Naughty Nick to help her feel as if she truly was Lovely Lucy?

The fumes from the wood stain must have been getting to Nick, because early Saturday evening he felt woozy. He only had about thirty minutes before he was supposed to leave Jenny's cabin and pick Lucy up. He wished he could call it quits early, but there was too much to be done and time was closing in.

When he finally reached the café, he spied Lucy waiting outside the entrance. While he appreciated she was standing there so he'd know he didn't need to hitch the horse across the lot and come inside to get her, he had lingering concerns about her being outside in such unseasonably cold weather.

"Are you sure you're ready for this?" he asked shortly before they reached the road leading to the pond.

"*Jah.* I love to skate."

"*Neh*, I mean, to, you know, pretend." Nick didn't want to say the words aloud again. He and Lucy had vaguely agreed they'd put on enough of a show to convince any naysayers they were courting, but they wouldn't be so obvious it would appear they were flaunting their courtship—which in their community would have been a dead giveaway they weren't really a couple. But Nick hadn't discussed the specifics with Lucy because she said if they orchestrated their behavior too much, they wouldn't come across as natural. With any other woman, Nick would have executed his role with ease, but with Lucy, he wasn't quite sure what to expect. Or what she expected of him.

Arriving at the rink together might have been a convincing indication they were courting were it not for the fact the Amish were scattered throughout Willow Creek's countryside, so many of the youth traveled together.

Eve spotted them right away. "Hi, Lucy. Hi, Nick," she greeted them, causing Melinda to glance up from where she wobbled across the ice, her ankles bending inward.

Nick and Lucy waved to both of them. They sat closely next to each other on one of the logs arranged like benches near the edge of the pond so they could lace their skates. Then they tentatively made their way across the frozen earth to the homemade rink.

Lucy stepped onto the ice first and within a few strokes she was gliding so gracefully it seemed as if she was born wearing skates. She had perfect balance. In choppier movements, Nick skated briskly up to her and said, "You're really *gut* at this. You have no fear."

"That's because I don't have far to fall," Lucy joked. "And because I've been skating since I was pretty young."

Nick laughed. "How is it you had to stay inside during recess but you were allowed to go ice skating?"

"It wasn't really that I was *allowed*," Lucy admitted. "It was that my *daed* didn't know about it. I'd use the skates Bridget had outgrown and the two of us would sneak off to the pond together. By the time my *daed* found out, I was a teenager and by then I was capable enough to convince him if I took it easy I could skate without losing my breath."

"Aha. That explains why you're kind of slow. Graceful, but slow," he taunted, and she whipped her scarf at him. He caught one end of it and asked, "Do you want a tow? Are you up for a little speed?"

"If you think you're strong enough to pull me, go ahead," she dared. He took off, pulling her in fast circles around the pond. She was shrieking and laughing, and he was laughing, too. Whoever else was on the rink, Nick didn't know; he only had eyes for Lucy.

"Okay, okay, I need a rest," she finally called, and he abruptly brought himself to a stop, holding out his arms to stop her, too. She glided right toward him, coming to a gentle stop beneath his chin. It was as if she fit perfectly there, and he dropped his arms to embrace her before she backed away. Although accidental, the public display of affection was more than most Amish youth demonstrated in public.

"How about some hot chocolate?" she suggested, gesturing across the lawn to where a bonfire was roaring.

"*Jah*, let's." They changed out of their skates and then Nick carried both pairs as they walked side by side to the bonfire. Lucy poured hot chocolate from one of the jugs someone had brought for the occasion and moved as close as she could to the fire.

Nick stood next to her, warmed through and through. The flames reflected off the front of her lenses, but from the side, he could see the corner of her eyes creased from her smile.

Suddenly, a deep voice questioned, "Lucy, is that

"FAST FIVE" READER SURVEY

Your participation entitles you to:
* Up to 4 FREE BOOKS and Thank-You Gifts Worth Over $20!

Complete the survey in minutes.

Romance

Suspense

Get Up to 4 **FREE Books**

Your Thank-You Gifts include up to **4 FREE BOOKS** and **2 MYSTERY GIFTS**. There's no obligation to purchase anything!

See inside for details.

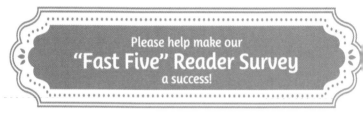

Dear Reader,

Since you are a lover of our books, your opinions are important to us... and so is your time.

That's why we made sure your **"FAST FIVE" READER SURVEY** can be completed in just a few minutes. Your answers to the five questions will help us remain at the forefront of women's fiction.

And, as a thank-you for participating, we'd like to send you up to **4 FREE BOOKS** and **FREE THANK-YOU GIFTS!**

Try **Love Inspired® Romance Larger-Print** books featuring Christian characters facing modern-day challenges.

Try **Love Inspired® Suspense Larger-Print** novels featuring Christian characters facing challenges to their faith... and lives.

Or TRY BOTH!

Enjoy your gifts with our appreciation,

Pam Powers

To get up to
4 FREE BOOKS & THANK-YOU GIFTS:

✻ Quickly complete the "Fast Five" Reader Survey
and return the insert.

"FAST FIVE" READER SURVEY

1	Do you sometimes read a book a second or third time?	○ Yes ○ No
2	Do you often choose reading over other forms of entertainment such as television?	○ Yes ○ No
3	When you were a child, did someone regularly read aloud to you?	○ Yes ○ No
4	Do you sometimes take a book with you when you travel outside the home?	○ Yes ○ No
5	In addition to books, do you regularly read newspapers and magazines?	○ Yes ○ No

YES! Please send me my Free Rewards, consisting of **2 Free Books from each series I select** and **Free Mystery Gifts**. I understand that I am under no obligation to buy anything, as explained on the back of this card.

❑ **Love Inspired® Romance Larger-Print** (122/322 IDL GNQY)
❑ **Love Inspired® Suspense Larger-Print** (107/307 IDL GNQY)
❑ **Try Both** (122/322 & 107/307 IDL GNRC)

FIRST NAME	LAST NAME

ADDRESS

APT.#	CITY

STATE/PROV.	ZIP/POSTAL CODE

you?" It was Dan, the young man from the soup kitchen. Despite Lucy's wish that Dan not discover their courtship, Nick found himself hoping the young man had seen them skating together. Or was it enough for Dan to see Nick and Lucy standing together like this in order to assume they were courting?

When Lucy grinned and replied, "Hi, Dan. I'm so glad to see you," Nick felt a stab of jealousy because she really did seem glad. "This is Nick."

That was all she said by way of introduction and Nick felt let down. Then someone nearby broke into song. Soon, everyone around the fire was singing Christmas carols, including Dan, whose singing voice was a rich baritone. Nick tried to recall what Lucy said about his own voice, but he couldn't. When she glanced his way and winked at him, he had to force himself to smile in return.

All the way home, Lucy raved about what a fun evening it was. "By the way, that little hug on the ice rink was a nice touch," she said. "I think we fooled everyone, don't you?"

Whether they fooled everyone or no one at all, Nick didn't care; he was consumed by the wish for their courtship to be as real as they were pretending it was.

Chapter Seven

"There was a skating party last night?" Mildred asked on the way home from church on Sunday. "Why didn't anyone tell us? Why didn't *you* tell us, Lucy?"

"You've always said you dislike being outdoors in the cold," Lucy explained, referencing the reason her stepsisters gave for needing to take the buggy instead of walking to their jobs. "Besides, you don't have skates."

"You should have let us know anyway. We could have hung out by the bonfire," Katura quibbled. "We haven't had any *schpass* all weekend. Not unless you consider helping our adolescent cousins bake four batches of sugar cookies for their school *Grischtdaag* pageant to be fun. Which I definitely do not."

Having met Mildred and Katura's cousins, Lucy couldn't argue. The young girls were notoriously messy, noisy and ill behaved. Lucy was glad her arrangement with Nick had spared her from spending late Saturday afternoon with them.

"At least there's a singing tonight," Mildred consoled Katura. To Lucy she said, "Are you and Nick going to that together, too?"

Lucy actually planned to stay home. It wasn't as if Nick could work on the repairs on the Sabbath. Besides, he'd mentioned his *ant* and *onkel* from Elmsville might be visiting their family after church and staying through supper, possibly overnight. "*Neh*, not this time. I think Nick has other plans."

Betty turned to face the three girls in the back seat. To Lucy she said, "It's wise of you to take a little break from Nick. Absence makes the heart grow fonder. And this way, you can go to the singing in the same buggy as Katura and Mildred."

"But I wasn't planning to go at all. I'm not in the caroling group," Lucy protested. She resented it when Betty pressured her to chaperone her stepsisters.

"That doesn't matter," Mildred insisted. "It's just like a regular Sunday singing, but we'll be singing carols to prepare for caroling. Everyone's invited."

"Maybe she's too tired," Lucy's father interjected from the front seat. "The Sabbath is meant to be a day of rest."

"If Lucy's that tired, she should limit her outings this week, too," Betty suggested. Lucy couldn't believe at her age her stepmother was still trying to control her activities, but she figured Betty was so used to doing it for her daughters she automatically did it for Lucy, too.

"I'm not too tired," Lucy argued. She didn't want anything standing in the way of her plans to be with Nick this week. "I'll go with Katura and Mildred."

The evening singing was held at the same place church had been held that morning—Doris and John Plank's house. After Jonas, Doris's stepson, led the three women to the large gathering room where the youth were hanging out, Doris approached and pulled

Lucy aside. She cupped her hands around Lucy's ear and whispered, "Nick is already here. He's over there, by Melinda."

Lucy's eyes darted to the far edge of the room. Melinda had literally backed Nick into a corner and, from the look on his face, he wasn't enjoying their discussion.

"I thought Nick wasn't going to be here, you little sneak," Katura jeered when she noticed Lucy staring. "No wonder you didn't put up your usual fight about coming with us."

Lucy didn't have the energy to insist she hadn't expected to see Nick that night. When Melinda suddenly moved away from Nick to make a beeline for Jonas, Lucy joined Nick in the corner.

"Lucy, hi!" He was smiling, but there was a tempestuous look in his otherwise bright blue eyes.

"Hi, Nick. I didn't expect to see you here tonight."

"I didn't expect to be here tonight, but I'm babysitting."

Lucy giggled. "I'm unofficially chaperoning, too. I thought Katura and Mildred were the only people who needed looking after. I didn't realize Kevin did, too."

"He doesn't—wait, I take that back. He does, but that's not why I'm here. I've been assigned to keep an eye on my cousins who are spending the night with us. But I've already lost track of them."

As Nick surveyed the room, grimacing, Lucy questioned, "Are you okay? I saw Melinda speaking to you and you seemed upset or something."

Instead of answering, Nick motioned toward the hall with his chin. "*Kumme* with me, okay?" Lucy followed as he led her from the room.

"What's wrong?" she asked again, and Nick explained how someone at church reportedly told Melinda he'd spotted Nick on the road to the Nelsons' cabin the previous afternoon. "It was around the time I supposedly would have been helping you accomplish some special *Grischtdaag* tasks you needed to do. Which I was, sort of, by bringing you to a quiet place so you could embroider, but, you know... Anyway, Melinda's nosiness has me concerned. I'm afraid somehow she's going to put two and two together. You and I are so close to completing our projects. I don't want her to spoil everything right at the very end."

Lucy saw red and she clenched her fists. "So what if some busybody spotted you alone in your buggy when you supposedly were spending time with me?" she fumed. "For all they know, you dropped me off at the mall so I could do some *Grischtdaag* shopping while you... I don't know, while you did shopping of your own. I'm not saying you should lie about it, of course, but that's just the point. There are infinite possibilities, none of which are anyone else's business. So why should you have to explain yourself to Melinda or anyone else?"

His eyes still stormy, Nick shook his head. "Melinda said she doesn't believe we're really a couple. And I think she's determined to prove it, Luce."

Nick had never called her Luce before and, despite her apprehension, Lucy was pleased by the familiarity of the nickname. "But she saw us together last night at the rink."

"Apparently, she wasn't convinced."

"Why does it matter to her anyway?" Lucy wondered aloud. "Is it because she's upset you turned Eve down?"

"It could be…" Nick hesitated. "Or maybe it's because, well, there was a time when Melinda and Jesse
were courting and they broke up for a while. During
that period, I walked out with Melinda. I quickly realized I didn't want to be her suitor, which she wasn't
too happy about. Ever since then, I've kind of had the
feeling she's been trying to get back at me."

Lucy stared at him, simultaneously trying to recon-
cile her annoyance at Melinda with her disappointment
in Nick. Didn't he have any discretion at all, to court
Melinda Schrock? For the first time, she understood
how Katura felt that Nick never asked *her* out—Lucy
felt the same way. She wondered what Melinda had
that Lucy didn't have—except a talent for gossiping.

Shaking her head, Lucy realized that was beside
the point at the moment. All that really mattered was
how desperately the soup kitchen needed funds. Lucy
was so close to finishing the tablecloth and napkins. If
she and Nick ended their pretense now, she wouldn't
be able to help raise funds, which would be like taking away hot meals from homeless people. And if Nick
couldn't finish his repairs, he'd be denying the Nelsons
the opportunity to enjoy one last family celebration in
a place they held dear.

"I've got a plan," she said, trembling. What she was
about to suggest was the most brazen idea she'd ever
expressed, but Lucy refused to allow anything to stand
in the way of accomplishing what she and Nick had
dedicated themselves to doing.

Nick couldn't guess how Lucy thought she could
remedy the situation, but he was willing to try anything.
He couldn't bear the thought of his father finding out

about Kevin's fire—or about Nick's involvement in the cleanup efforts. He shuddered to think how his father's health might suffer, at Christmastime no less. But Nick doubted there was any convincing Melinda, for once and for all, that he and Lucy were truly a couple.

"What is it?" he asked.

Lucy bit her lip. *Does she even have a plan?* Nick wondered. She looked downward as she wrung her hands, speaking so quietly he could hardly hear her. "We'll stay out here talking until Melinda walks by. She'll see we're spending time alone together. She'll see how close we're standing."

"She saw that last night, too, but it didn't convince her." Nick was losing hope.

"*Jah*, but tonight when she walks by, you're going to…" Lucy waved her hand about her lips.

He couldn't hear what she said, and he didn't understand what she was supposed to be miming. "I'm going to what?" he asked.

Averting her eyes, she pulled on the strings of her prayer *kapp*. "You're going to kiss me."

Nick's legs felt rubbery and he couldn't speak.

"Suddenly, I mean. As if we don't think anyone is watching and you're stealing a kiss," she explained, her cheeks flaming. Her ears were, too.

Her abashment was endearing but it was also contagious. Nick had never been so nervous in his life. Not even with his first kiss. "Okay," he said, and placed his hand on Lucy's shoulder.

Flinching, she huffed, "What are you doing?"

"I'm… I'm getting ready," he hemmed and hawed. "It—it will look more natural if I have my hand on your shoulder. You know, like I'm sort of leading up to kissing you." Upon saying the words "kissing you," Nick's mouth went dry.

"Oh, okay." Lucy allowed him to put his hand on her shoulder again. He could feel the angular bone of her clavicle beneath his thumb. "Should I take my glasses off?"

"*Neh*, that won't look spontaneous enough."

"Right," she whispered, nodding. "Let me know when Melinda comes by."

Because he could easily see over Lucy's head, Nick had a clear view through the entryway into the gathering room. They didn't have to wait long until someone clapped his hands to get everyone's attention, a signal the singing would soon commence. Nick figured it was a matter of seconds before Melinda came out looking for them.

"It won't be long now," he said as his stomach jittered. From beneath lowered eyelids, he peeked at Lucy, whose face was level with his chest, to behold her fine bone structure. Someone who was meeting her for the first time might have mistaken her for a much younger teen, but once you spoke with Lucy, you could never again see her as anything other than a bright, self-possessed and skillful woman. *How did I miss so many qualities in her?* Nick mused. A shadow crossed the door, and Nick immediately used his knuckle to tilt Lucy's chin toward him. He bent forward, his mouth hovering over hers.

"Sorry, false alarm. It was Doris," he said when he realized his mistake. His lips nearly touched hers with each syllable he pronounced.

Lucy smiled. "It might have been just as effective

to have Doris see us as to have Melinda see us," she said, just as Melinda stepped into the hall.

Nick didn't have time to warn Lucy before he brushed his lips against hers. Their skin barely made contact long enough for him to feel the plush softness of her mouth before she drew back. He felt like a thousand hummingbirds were darting through his veins as his gaze lingered on her. In that moment, he couldn't have cared less about whether Melinda had seen them or not. It wouldn't have mattered if Lucy and Nick's entire plan failed and Melinda exposed their charade that very evening. Kissing Lucy was worth ten times the amount of trouble Nick would get into if his parents ever found out about the cabin.

When Melinda cleared her throat loudly, Nick turned his attention to her. She had thrust her hands on her hips. "There you two are," she said. Her voice registered annoyance, indicating she had indeed witnessed the kiss. "We're about to start singing and Dan said he heard about our group from you, Lucy, so I thought you two might want to share a songbook."

Nick had been so intent on watching Melinda's reaction to the kiss he completely missed noticing Dan, who was shifting from foot to foot behind her. "Hi, Lucy. Nick," he said awkwardly.

Appearing flustered, Lucy pivoted toward Dan and Melinda and gushed, "Dan, I'm so glad you could *kumme*. Let's go into the other room. After the singing Nick and I will introduce you to everyone."

Nick's elation was quickly replaced by a crush of disappointment. His legs felt wooden as he followed Lucy and Dan into the gathering room. After they took seats in chairs arranged around the periphery of the room, Nick kept ruminating on the fact that Lucy had invited Dan to the singing. When? At the soup kitchen? Or had she told him about it today at church? For a fleeting second, Nick's imagination ran away with him, and he wondered if Lucy had actually proposed the kiss to make *Dan* jealous.

No, that couldn't be. Lucy hadn't even been aware that Nick thought Melinda was on the verge of figuring out their secret until he told Lucy that evening. The kiss *had* to be Lucy's spontaneous plot to throw Melinda off, not a planned one for Dan's benefit. *I've got to get a grip*, Nick thought. But no sooner had he put one worry to rest than another one popped up in its place: Was Lucy only biding her time with Nick until they'd completed their respective Christmas projects? Was it her hope that after Christmas Dan would offer to be her suitor?

As the others lifted their voices around him, Nick decided he couldn't let that happen. No, he had to extend the length of the project at the cabin. He wasn't ready to let Lucy go just yet.

Although Mildred and Katura dropped off almost as soon as their heads hit their pillows on Sunday night, Lucy couldn't sleep, so she gathered her embroidery materials and crept downstairs. She still had to finish two more place mats for the special order Joseph Schrock had requested. She turned on a lamp and snuggled beneath a quilt, but she couldn't focus on embroidering. All she could think about was the kiss she'd shared with Nick. Never in a million years would she have imagined herself suggesting such a thing, but now she was so glad she had. As momentary as their kiss had been, it was the most powerful physical sensation she'd ever experienced and a shudder racked her body as she thought about Nick's thick, full lips skimming her own, her shoulder warm beneath the weight of his palm.

Of course, the kiss wasn't real. It was just for effect. No matter how many times she reminded herself of that, Lucy couldn't squelch the sensation of pure bliss at the memory. She would rather share one fake kiss with Nick than a thousand real kisses with…well, with anyone else.

How she wished their time together wasn't coming to an end. She felt like the fictional Cinderella character she'd read about in books from the *Englisch* library; at the stroke of midnight, her dream would vanish. Unless… She allowed herself to wonder if Nick would ever consider courting her for real.

But that thought was preposterous. Nick had been tolerant about her physical shortcomings, but that's because he stood to benefit from their arrangement. Lucy knew she wasn't "marriage material," as the saying went. Men wanted robust women; they wanted women who could bear half a dozen healthy children. At the very least, they wanted wives who weren't too feeble to go outdoors to beat a rug or sweep the porch. Besides, she and Nick were polar opposites, so it was useless to allow herself to hope Nick was interested in her romantically, wasn't it? She wished she had someone to confide in about the situation. If only she could write to Bridget for advice. But in a way, Lucy already knew what Bridget's advice would be: she'd tell her to steer clear of Nick. To save herself a world of heartache.

Any heartache is worth how elated I feel right now,

Lucy thought before she finally dozed off, wishing she could slumber straight through until Wednesday night, when Nick would take her to the soup kitchen again. But she woke the next morning to a draft of cool air followed by a loud click and then her father's footsteps tapping down the porch stairs. She wished she hadn't missed preparing breakfast for him once again. She sat up and blinked, realizing she should rise before Betty entered the room. Too late.

"Why did you sleep on the sofa, Lucy? Are you ill?" Betty asked.

Why did everyone always assume she was sick? "*Neh.* I felt like I couldn't sleep last night so I came down here to embroider for a while. I don't remember what happened after that, but the next thing I knew, it was morning." Actually, Lucy did recall thinking about Nick, but those thoughts felt more like a dream than something she'd willed herself to consider. They were too private to mention to Betty, anyway. "I'll put the *kaffi* on," Lucy volunteered.

To her surprise, Betty insisted she'd do it instead while Lucy gingerly gathered her embroidery and combed her hair. Betty served the hot beverage at the table along with eggs and bacon, but Lucy could hardly eat.

"Are you sure you're not coming down with something?" Betty asked.

This time Lucy snapped, "*Neh.* Why does everyone always assume I'm sick?"

Betty looked taken aback, and Lucy regretted her tone immediately. Her stepmother probably was worried, just as Nick expressed he'd been. "I'm sorry," Lucy apologized. "I know you're concerned about my health. But I'm not sick."

"Yet you still can't eat?" A smile played on Betty's lips as she blew on her coffee. "That happened to me, too, when your *daed* first began courting me. I couldn't eat, I couldn't sleep. Lovesickness is all it is."

Inwardly, Lucy groaned. She almost felt bad that Betty was so hopeful about her courtship with Nick, knowing the disappointment her stepmother would experience when they broke up in another week or so. "It's more likely I ate too many brownies last night, not that I'm lovesick."

"Oh, but she *is* lovesick!" Mildred chanted from the doorway. She was still dressed in her bedclothes. "She and Nick were hiding in the hallway kissing last night."

"Mildred!" Betty scolded, genuinely angry. "That's none of your business and it's inappropriate to talk about."

"It was even less appropriate for her to do it in public view." Katura was suddenly in the room. She slunk into a chair and poured herself a cup of coffee.

"It doesn't sound as if she was in public view," Betty said as she rose to get eggs for her daughters. Lucy was amazed her stepmother was standing up for her, but at the same time she wanted to cringe. Lucy and Nick hadn't wanted everyone to know about the kiss—just Melinda. But they should have known she'd tell everyone else, too. It had been embarrassing enough that Dan had witnessed the kiss firsthand without everyone else being given a secondhand account.

Betty continued to scold her daughters. "Do I need to remind you of what the Bible says about envy?"

"Envy? Pah!" Katura muttered, loud enough so

Lucy could hear but not so loud that Betty turned from the stove. "That courtship isn't going to last. With Nick, it never does. Mark my words, within a month, he'll have moved on to someone else."

To Lucy, it almost sounded like wishful thinking on Katura's part. But her stepsister was right; before the month was up, Lucy's arrangement with Nick would be over. *I'm not looking forward to bearing the humiliation of listening to Katura gloat.* But even worse, Lucy would have to bear the pain of ending her courtship. Right then and there, she decided until that day came, she was going to make the most of her time with Nick while she had it.

Nick could hardly wait to take Lucy to the soup kitchen. It felt like forever since he'd seen her. Since he'd kissed her. If only someone else needed convincing they were really a couple… He shook his head. Was he really that pathetic he'd daydream about excuses to steal another fake kiss from Lucy instead of being brave enough to ask if she'd ever allow him an authentic one? The answer, sadly, was yes. His courtship—and his kiss—with Lucy might have been contrived, but they were better than nothing. Which was exactly what he'd be left with if Lucy turned down his proposal to become her suitor for real.

"I heard you were really putting on a show with Lucy at the singing last night," Kevin remarked on Monday as they stacked bags of deicing material in a bin by the door before the store opened. Supposedly, snow was on its way, and their customers would need to treat their driveways and sidewalks.

Regardless of the public nature of his kiss with

Lucy, Nick resented his brother's intrusive remark so he ignored it entirely.

"It can't be easy, pretending to like her. I just want you to know how much I appreciate what you're doing for me," Kevin added in a rare display of gratitude.

"It's not a problem. I like spending time with Lucy," Nick said, suddenly defensive. "She's…she's different than most women I've courted."

"You can say that again," Kevin said.

Now Nick was even more irked. "What exactly does that mean anyway?"

"Well, Lucy's sort of plain. She'd kind of, you know, dull."

"That just goes to show how little you know her," Nick said. "And how little you know about the other women I've courted. All that external facade, the animated conversations, the flirty gestures, the exaggerated giggling—*that* gets boring pretty quickly." Nick was articulating feelings he hadn't fully realized he had.

Kevin cocked his head. "All right, fess up. Are you and Lucy really a couple now or what?"

"Of course not. What makes you say that?"

"From the way you're talking about her. And from what Melinda described—"

"Melinda has big mouth and so do you, so you'd better shut it before you stick your foot in it."

"Okay, okay," Kevin said, holding his hands up. "How long until you're done with the cabin anyway?"

If Nick wanted to, he could finish up in about three more nights. But he didn't want to. "I've got a little sanding left to do. A couple more pieces of paneling to get right before I hang them. And of course there's the cleanup. I accidentally scuffed up the floor in a few places when I was moving furniture around, so I'll want to buff that, too."

"I know how to do those things. I could take over and you could tend the store at night."

Nick panicked. It was true; Kevin could handle those tasks on his own. "*Neh*, I started the project, I'll finish it."

"Because you want to spend more time with Lucy?"

"Because I don't trust you to get the job done."

But Kevin was right. Nick did want to spend more time with Lucy. As he sped to her house, an idea struck him: he'd help her serve at the soup kitchen. That way, his project would be extended one more evening and he'd get to spend additional time with her. More to the point, she wouldn't be spending time alone with Dan. Nick couldn't wait to propose the idea to her. Since Dan had witnessed them "kissing," as well as at the rink, Lucy couldn't argue there was a need to hide their courtship from him any longer.

"Oh, if you can spare the time that would be *wunderbaar*," she said when Nick presented his idea. "We're shorthanded because people have so many other commitments at this time of year. We need a few men to help set up the folding tables beforehand and carry the heavier trays during the meal. Then there's bussing the tables afterward. Dan does a lot of that, but he can't handle it all on his own. Although he sure tries. He's one of the hardest workers there, which is saying a lot since everyone is so dedicated."

At the mention of Dan's name, Nick's mouth soured. Lucy always seemed to praise him, and Nick was desperate to find out if she was interested in him romantically. "He seemed really glad to see you the other night," he hinted.

"*Jah*, well, since he's new in the next district I've been trying to get him to attend a singing. He's kind of shy. Or I guess you'd call him socially reserved, like me. Which is probably why we work so well together. Anyway, I was glad to see him at the Planks' last night. I think meeting a few people at the rink on Saturday helped him feel more comfortable about attending a singing, too. You wouldn't know this because you're so outgoing, but for us introverted types, well, let's just say social events aren't usually high on our list of things we love to do."

Her response did nothing to quell Nick's envy. To hear her talk about them, Lucy and Dan were perfectly compatible: both hard workers, both quiet. Dan was probably smart like Lucy was, too, and clearly he was charitable. Nick almost wished he hadn't offered to help serve on Wednesday night, because he didn't know if he could stand to witness the rapport between Lucy and Dan as they worked.

But when they arrived at the soup kitchen, there was no time for wallowing. The *Englischers* greeted him with gratitude and huge smiles. Then the place was bustling. Nick could hardly set up additional chairs and clear the tables fast enough to keep the crowd comfortable and content.

And Lucy... Well, Lucy was a force to be reckoned with. Nick knew she was industrious, but he hadn't realized quite how much energy such a small person could generate. She prepared sandwiches, served food, poured beverages and wiped up spills, yet he noticed she always had time to stop and chat with the diners, smiling all the while. Watching her, Nick smiled, too. And as a local church choir sang Christmas carols in the background, he found himself humming along. *At least I can hum in tune to the music*, he thought, chuckling at his own expense.

When most of the diners had left and Lucy was carrying a tray of glasses across the room, Nick noticed it was tipping precariously to her left. He hurried across the room to assist her, but Dan beat him to it. Nick noticed Dan's hands dwarfed Lucy's as he up righted the tray before taking it from her.

"*Denki*, Dan," she said. "That was close."

Yeah, too close, Nick thought begrudgingly. He didn't want envy gnawing at his gut, but he felt outdone. Dan was truly a generous and compassionate guy, serving others regularly, whereas Nick was just pretending to help a family in need. Of course, Lucy didn't know that and Nick intended to make sure she never found out. Otherwise, he wouldn't stand a chance against Dan for Lucy's affections.

Realizing he had to maximize his time with her, on the way home Nick finally worked up the courage to say to Lucy, "I'd like to pick you up early on Friday night, if that's okay. I thought maybe we could get a pizza or something before I drop you off at the café."

"Oh, sure," Lucy agreed breezily. Nick's self-esteem momentarily soared until she added, "I understand why you want to get an earlier start on your project. I do, too. We've been keeping some awfully late hours, haven't we? But there's no need for us to go out for supper. I'll pack something we can eat along the way."

That wasn't at all what Nick had in mind, but he was too embarrassed to tell Lucy he wanted to take her out to supper for the pleasure of taking her out to supper, so he just agreed with her idea. Next time, he'd be more forthright. *If there is a next time*, he thought, all too aware their arrangement was one day closer to drawing to an end.

Chapter Eight

Even though the temperature was in the high twenties, Lucy waited on the porch for Mildred and Katura to return from working at the mercantile on Thursday. When their buggy pulled up the lane, she dashed across the lawn so as soon as they disembarked she could take the reins and head back to town. That afternoon she'd finished embroidering the last of the place mats she'd promised to deliver to Schrock's before the shop closed. To her delight, the customer who had ordered them was eagerly awaiting Lucy's arrival.

"Lucy Knepp, I'd like to introduce you to Sandra Nelson," Joseph said.

"Oh, they're exquisite, just as I knew they would be!" the woman exclaimed after Lucy spread the place mats on the counter for her to examine. "I can't tell you how much this means to me. We're having a special Christmas celebration this year at our family's cabin for my father who's visiting us from Washington State. I'm probably going overboard with the preparations, but I want to create as festive a setting as I can. These are going to look lovely."

Lucy had been so intent on showing the customer the finished product she hadn't paid attention to the woman's last name. But when Sandra Nelson described her family's upcoming celebration, Lucy caught her breath. *This is the same Nelson family whose cabin Nick is working on!* she realized, utterly thrilled. *I can't wait to tell him about this happenstance!*

"Here you go, Mrs. Nelson," Melinda said from behind Lucy. She set two large red cinnamon-scented candles on the counter. "I guess we did have a couple of these in the back room after all."

"Oh, thank you, Melinda," Sandra replied. Carefully stacking the place mats, she said, "Everything is falling into place beautifully. Look at what Lucy just brought me, too."

Melinda barely glanced at Lucy's handiwork. "Did you say you're having a party at the cabin? That must mean it's all fixed up now."

"All fixed up? Hardly! I've collected most of the embellishments, but I haven't begun to decorate. In fact, I haven't even given the place a thorough cleaning yet. Because of my work schedule, that won't happen until next week. But I'm not worried about it, not at all," Sandra quipped, chuckling nervously.

Melinda began to clarify her question, saying, "*Neh*, I wasn't asking if you'd decorated yet, I meant has the cabin been—"

Aware Melinda must have heard about the fire and, mortified that she was about to let the cat out of the bag, Lucy had to act quickly. Since she couldn't think of any other way to butt in, she began coughing violently into the crook of her elbow. It was a phony cough at first, but the more she coughed the more she legitimately had to cough, and soon she was gasping. Mrs. Nelson patted her back as Joseph directed Melinda to bring Lucy a cup of water.

After catching her breath, Lucy said, "I'm sorry about that. Don't worry, I'm not contagious. I have asthma, that's all. I never know what's going to set it off." Lucy wasn't lying—the scented candles may have exacerbated her breathing difficulty. "I think I'll go see if Melinda has that glass of water. I'm so pleased I got to meet you and I hope you have a joyful celebration."

"We will," Sandra said. "Thanks in part to you, Lucy."

When she located Melinda in the back room, Lucy did her best to trap her there until she was sure Mrs. Nelson had left the shop.

"Denki," Lucy said, slowly sipping her third cup. "I don't know quite what triggered that coughing attack, but I feel much better now."

"The cold weather is probably too much for your delicate constitution," Melinda commented. "I heard it's going to snow tomorrow night, so if you were planning to go out, you might want to think twice. You don't want to catch a cold."

Aware her peers planned to socialize after rehearsing carols, Lucy was antagonized by Melinda's remark. She and Nick wouldn't have wanted to attend the party anyway, but it was insulting that Melinda was clearly trying to stop her. "I don't think the weather has anything to do with it. Nick always brings extra blankets to keep me toasty warm. If I am coming down with something, it's more likely I caught it from... I don't know, from sitting too close to someone who had a cold at church. Or something like that."

Lucy's thinly veiled reference to kissing Nick didn't

escape Melinda's notice. Her eyes narrowed and she screwed her mouth into a frown, but for once she was speechless. Satisfied, Lucy followed her back into the main gallery, where she was happy to discover Sandra Nelson had left. *As long as she doesn't* kumme *back before* Grischtdaag, *my secret with Nick is safe,* Lucy thought.

Then she decided if Melinda was right about Friday's forecast, sandwiches wouldn't suffice for supper; Lucy would prepare a hot meal to take in thermal containers. So the next day she prepared *yumasetta* with rolls and "stained glass window" cookies—a favorite Christmas treat made from chocolate, walnuts and marshmallows—for dessert. It would be too awkward eating as they traveled, but Lucy figured she could give Nick his share to take with him to the cabin. Or, preferably, he could spare a few minutes to eat with her in the buggy before dropping her off for the evening.

"You're going on a picnic?" Mildred asked when she saw Lucy packing a basket. "In December?"

"Wow, I never knew Nick was so cheap," Katura added. "It's a *gut* thing he never asked to be my suitor. I wouldn't have abided by someone who couldn't even treat me to supper."

"It's not because he's cheap," Lucy said protectively. "It's because he has to work on the—" She stopped herself just in time. This wasn't the first instance when her temper had caused her to speak rashly. She ducked into the pantry hoping to change the subject. "Do we have any paper napkins?" she asked.

"Second shelf," Katura answered. "Nick has to work on what?"

Lucy feigned innocence. "Hmm?"

"You started to say Nick had to work on something tonight. I thought the two of you were going out."

"We are," Lucy insisted. "But we want to eat on the way because we're, uh... We're going to be on the road for a while to get to where...where we want to go—and before you ask me, I'm not going to tell you where that is. I deserve some privacy, you know."

Now Lucy's father emerged from the mudroom. Lucy hadn't heard him come in. "At the risk of invading that privacy, what do you mean you're going to be on the road for a while? It's only flurrying out there now, but it might keep up."

"*Jah*, but horses can maneuver much better in the snow than cars can."

"Exactly. That's why I don't want you on the road with the cars."

Entering the room, Betty asked, "Do you think it's too slick for the girls to go out tonight?"

Katura, Mildred and Lucy simultaneously voiced their protests until Marvin grumpily conceded. Lucy planted a kiss on his cheek. "*Denki* for thinking about our safety, *Daed*, but we won't take any unnecessary risks and we're in the Lord's care."

Marvin hugged his daughter and replied, "Nick had *better* not take any unnecessary risks with you or he'll have to answer to me." Then he shuffled into the parlor to read while Betty began setting the table so they could eat the meal Lucy had prepared.

"Nick won't take any risks?" Betty shook her head. "That would be a first. Unless you've already tamed him, Lucy."

Lucy was indignant. "He's not a wild horse!"

"*Neh*, but you're so sensible I figured maybe some of it rubbed off on him."

Although Lucy suspected her stepmother was giving her a compliment, once again she felt like she was being called boring. But, since she'd gotten her way about going out, she shrugged it off and went to change her cape and apron. She was so eager for Nick to arrive she waited outside so she could see his horse coming up the lane.

Nick whistled as he sped toward Lucy's house on Friday evening, again grateful for how swiftly Penny cantered, despite the light coating of snow on the roads. After leaving work, Nick had made a quick stop at the *Englisch* candy shop, where he bought a box of Christmas candy for Lucy. Since she'd prepared their supper, the least he wanted to do was get her something special for dessert.

He selected an assortment of the kinds of treats they used to receive after their childhood Christmas pageants at school, including peppermint bark, Christmas tree nougats, peanut brittle, chocolate-covered orange slices and ribbon candy. The school performances traditionally included singing hymns and carols—even then Nick only mouthed the words—and reciting the Bible Nativity story from memory. Afterward, each child always received a small but treasured box of candy from their teacher and the school board.

As Nick recalled, Lucy usually had the longest passage of Scripture to recite and he even remembered one year his parents remarked what a clear voice she'd used; they were surprised someone so small could project so well. That same year, he'd witnessed two of his older friends snatch Lucy's box of candy when she set it down on the landing near the entrance of the school so she could dash back inside to retrieve her scarf. Nick had been certain he'd be accused of taking it, since he was nearby when it happened, but he had hesitated to squeal on his friends. Upon returning, Lucy's expression had wilted when she discovered her box missing, but apparently she never said a word about it to anyone. Or if she did, Nick never found out.

I hope she still likes peppermint bark, he thought as he spied her loitering on the porch. He halted the buggy quickly and jumped out to help her with the cumbersome basket she was carrying. Since romantic relationships were supposedly private, it wasn't a custom for young suitors to go inside the houses of the women they were courting, but Nick wished Lucy didn't always wait outside for him. It made him wonder if she didn't want her father to see her in Nick's company. Everyone knew Marvin Knepp was as upright and respected a man as could be, and Nick hoped he approved of Nick courting his daughter.

What am I thinking? I'm not courting Lucy! Nick reminded himself as he aided her into the buggy. Once they were situated, she began telling him about how she'd run into Sandra Nelson in Schrock's Shop.

"Can you believe it?" Lucy exclaimed. "Isn't that odd that we're both indirectly involved with helping the Nelsons have a happy *Grischtdaag* celebration? Of course, I got paid for my efforts, whereas you're doing yours out of true generosity."

Even though he was wearing gloves, Nick reflexively wiped his palms against his lap. "You didn't, uh, say anything to her, did you? I mean, let on you knew I was making the repairs?"

Lucy turned toward him, crinkling her forehead. "Of course not. Why would I do that? But it's a *gut* thing I was there because Melinda Schrock started questioning Mrs. Nelson about whether the cabin would be ready in time. I didn't realize Melinda knew there'd been a fire. Although I guess that shouldn't surprise me."

Nick's pulse drummed like hoofbeats in his ears. "So Melinda mentioned the fire to Mrs. Nelson?"

"She started to, but don't worry. I cut her off." Lucy giggled. "I suddenly developed a terrific coughing fit. Melinda had to get me a cup of water, and I cornered her in the back room until Mrs. Nelson left the shop."

Nick's shoulders relaxed, but only a little. He wasn't merely worried about Mrs. Nelson finding out about the fire—he was worried Lucy would learn the fire was Kevin's fault. Melinda hadn't been at the party that night, but by now word had probably gotten around that there'd been a fire. Granted, as long as Kevin kept his mouth shut, none of the Amish would know Nick was the one making the repairs, but Nick couldn't allow Lucy to find out that he hadn't been entirely forthcoming with her in the first place. What would she think of him if she knew he wasn't really as helpful or as generous as she thought he was?

"Melinda didn't say anything else?" he questioned.

"*Neh*, I didn't even let her finish her sentence, so Mrs. Nelson's none the wiser." Lucy gave his arm a nudge. "Why are you being such a nervous Nellie?"

Nick released a big sigh. "I don't know. I guess I

wonder how Melinda found out about the fire, that's all."

"Who knows? I don't think much gets past her," Lucy said.

"*Jah*, that's why it was perfect when we were kissing at the Planks' *haus*. I mean, it was perfect Melinda was the one who saw us. It wasn't perfect that we were kissing. I mean, there wasn't anything wrong with our kiss, just—" The fact he'd even referenced their kissing aloud made Nick so flustered he couldn't recover enough to complete his thought.

Fortunately, Lucy was gracious enough to say, "It's okay, I know what you meant. Our plan worked perfectly, and I think Melinda finally accepts it that we're courting."

Even if we're not, Nick thought, but he bit the inside of his cheek. He didn't want to make a bigger fool of himself than he already had.

"Do you want to take a few minutes to eat here in the buggy?" Lucy asked when they pulled into the parking lot by the café. "I probably shouldn't bring food inside. Besides, it's so pretty with the snow. I always think the first snowfall is the prettiest."

"That would be *wunderbaar*," Nick agreed. His stomach was rumbling. Or were those very loud butterflies?

"I hope you like *yumasetta* because—" Lucy stopped midsentence and pointed at the darkened building. "Look. The lights are out. It can't be closed. It's Friday night."

Nick squinted. It was definitely dark inside the café. He climbed down to read the sign posted in the window. When he returned he explained, "The café is closed because they're having a staff *Grischtdaag* party off-site."

"Oh, *neh*," Lucy protested. Then she suggested, "I suppose I could sit in the fast-food restaurant down the road. I think they'll let me stay for a few hours if I buy something, won't they?"

Nick was skeptical about the shabby little restaurant. He didn't want to take the chance someone there might harass Lucy. "I could take you to the bookstore on the border of Highland Springs," he suggested.

"That's miles away. You'll lose any time you may have saved by picking me up early."

Nick rubbed his chin. His face felt chapped from the raw wind. Lucy was sniffling from the cold, too. "If you're willing you could *kumme* to the cabin with me. I've cleaned up the sawdust and I only have some very light sanding to do. It's warm inside and we can have supper there. That is, unless you'll find the noise too distracting."

The noise? That was the least of Lucy's distractions. Nick's earlier reference to their kissing had made it nearly impossible for Lucy to speak coherently all the way here, and it was still flitting through her mind. She had to keep focused.

"That sounds like a *gut* plan. This way, you can work as late as you need to because you won't have to worry about the café closing at ten." Lucy's stomach was twirling circles. Somehow eating at the cabin with Nick felt much closer to being courted than eating in the buggy. But she reminded herself it was a far cry from him actually taking her out for supper, as Katura had indirectly pointed out.

"Great. Just one more dilemma," Nick said. "I can either keep Penny to an even trot, in which case, we might be cold by the time we get there because it will take longer. Or, I can push her to a run, in which case we'll get there faster but we'll definitely be colder along the way from the breeze. Which do you prefer?"

"Do you really have to ask?"

Grinning, Nick pushed his hat farther down on his head and lifted the reins. And then they were sailing, their momentum matching the elation of Lucy's mood. With the snow falling around them the scenery was so pristine and romantic Lucy felt like she was dreaming. Only this was better, because she wasn't.

At the house Nick switched on the lights. "I don't like to turn up their heat when I'm here, but I'm happy to build a fire."

"Great," Lucy said. "While you're doing that, I'll get our supper ready. How about if we eat here on the floor in front of the fireplace? I'm chilly."

"It will be like a picnic," Nick agreed.

He made the room cozy warm in no time and then removed two oversize pillows from the sofa for Lucy and him to sit on. She asked him to say grace and when he was finished, she served him a heaping plate of *yumasetta*. Whatever awkwardness she had felt earlier dissipated as she dug into the hot meal. She was finishing her second helping of the meaty casserole and her third roll when Nick laughed.

"What's so funny?" she asked.

"For someone so petite, you sure can pack it in!" he guffawed.

Lucy blushed. She'd been called *short* before and she'd been called a *shrimp*. Once someone even referred to her as a *runt*. But somehow having a man call her petite felt... Well, it made her feel more feminine. It made her feel womanly instead of girlish.

"I haven't even gotten started on dessert yet," she admitted.

"Ach! Dessert! I'll be right back." Nick dashed out the door without his coat and returned clutching a large gold box tied with a satiny red bow. "For you."

Eagerly Lucy untied the ribbon and lifted the lid to find peanut brittle and gumdrops, ribbon candy and peppermint bark. "These are all my favorites," she said, suddenly self-conscious that he'd given her a gift. "We always used to get a little box of these after our school *Grischtdaag* pageants."

"That's why I got them," Nick admitted without the slightest hesitation. "To remind you of when we were young."

Lucy laughed. "Most people would say we're still young." She extended the box to Nick so he could take a piece, but a shadow crossed his face and he shook his head, refusing the candy.

"I was there the night Noah and Nathan Miller took yours when you went back into the schoolhouse to collect your belongings."

Lucy didn't know what he was talking about. Then it occurred to her, something she had to dig into the hazy recess of her memory to recall. "Oh, those poor *buwe*," she lamented.

"Poor *buwe*? They stole from you."

"*Jah*, but they ended up getting tummy aches and missing *Grischtdaag* dinner. Or so their *mamm* told me when she brought them over to apologize a few days later."

"That's justice well deserved," Nick said. "But I should talk. I got off scot-free. I saw what they did, and I didn't stop them or speak up."

"They were older than you and they were your friends. Stopping them or tattling would have been a difficult thing for a young *bu* to do."

"I imagine the way they acted was difficult for *you*," Nick lamented.

He looked so guilt-stricken Lucy felt bad for him. Shrugging, she said, "It was only candy. Besides, this more than makes up for it—look how many pieces are in here!"

Nick laughed, but Lucy was being genuine. She offered the box to him again, but he shook his head a second time. "Those are for you. You don't need to share. Besides, I'm so full if I eat another bite I won't be able to move and I've got work to do."

"You go ahead and get started, and I'll clean this up," Lucy said, motioning to their dishes. When she was finished, she asked if he'd prefer her to work in another room. She didn't want to crowd him.

"I think you should stay here where it's warm. Unless the noise bothers you."

Touched by how thoughtful he was about her comfort, Lucy snuggled onto one end of the sofa beneath a bright light. The cabin's electric lights shone brighter than the gaslamps in her home, affording her more precision as she embroidered. Even so, Lucy probably accomplished only half as much as she normally might have. She kept stopping to steal glances at Nick as he worked.

His hands were so capable and strong. She noticed he was something of a perfectionist, sanding a board and then eyeing the edge before sanding it a little more. He used the same meticulous approach when hanging the boards, too. She'd always known he was an energetic person, but until she observed him working, she hadn't realized how patient he was. Watching him work was so mesmerizing she kept losing track of her stitching.

"What's wrong?" he asked at one point, a couple hours later. "You're frowning."

"Am I? I was just thinking about how... I don't know, how I've misjudged you. Or I did in the past. I thought you were this impulsive, careless *bu*, but come to find out, you're actually quite thoughtful and particular and dedicated. I was really wrong. I suppose that's why the Lord doesn't want us to judge one another."

Nick experienced a rush of pleasure and an equal amount of guilt over Lucy's comments. On one hand, he was pleased by her compliments. On the other, he didn't truly live up to her revised version of him, either. After all, he hadn't been forthright about the reason behind the renovation.

"You probably judged me pretty accurately," he said. "Just ask my *eldre* what I was like as a *kind*."

Setting aside her embroidery, Lucy said, "Well, maybe in the past, when we were *kinner*, but not now. Not anymore." Standing, she stretched and she reminded him of a cat. A kitten. Then she walked over to his side and studied the wall as if looking at a sunset. "Your work is beautiful. How did you ever get the colors to match like that?"

Nick's throat felt as if he'd swallowed a handful of pebbles. He was coming unhinged by her praise and her presence. "I had help. Hunter Schwartz gave me some hints."

"You told him about the project?"

"*Neh*, I just asked him a few general questions about staining. I haven't told anyone about the project. You're the only one who knows," he said.

"Except for the Nelson *bu*," she reminded him.

Nick looked askance at her. "The Nelson *bu*?"

"*Jah, schnickelfritz*, the Nelson *bu*. You know, your friend whose family owns this cabin." She angled her head up toward him, a saucy grin on her face. He knew he ought to correct her assumption, to tell her his friend was a female named Jenny, but somehow, all he could think about was removing her glasses and kissing her eyebrows, which rose in perfect arcs right above her lenses.

Suddenly afraid she could tell what he was thinking, he said, "You've seen my work, now can I see yours?"

The palest pink tinged her face. "Sure, if you really want to."

She walked to the sofa and held up her embroidery hoop. Fastened within it was a linen napkin on which she'd embroidered an intricate snowflake pattern of white on white, with a hint of gold thread here and there. It reminded him exactly of how the snow looked falling in the moonlight outside the window.

He whistled. "Whoa. Someone's going to bid a lot for a set of those."

She bit her lip skeptically. "I hope so. I like it, but I'm afraid the *Englischers* won't. Most of them tend to prefer more colorful patterns. But I chose this one because...well, because I think it's beautiful in a surprising way. I mean it has a quiet kind of beauty, if you have eyes to see it."

"I know exactly what you mean," Nick said. And he did know, because what Lucy just said described exactly how he felt about her beauty. It was quietly winsome and true, not flashy or bold. He licked his lips, but as much as he wanted to, he couldn't kiss her. Not without asking to be her suitor for real, first. And he couldn't do that unless he was sure she felt the same way about him as he did about her. Never before had the possibility of rejection scared him so much. When he asked to court women in the past, he always leaped in, feet first, instead of weighing the consequences. *Am I becoming more mature or just overly cautious?*

Lucy sighed and said, "Well, either way, it's too late now."

"What's too late?"

"It's too late to change my pattern. I have to turn it in on Thursday. That's only six days away. But thanks to our arrangement, I'll meet the deadline. It looks as if you're going to finish on time, too."

The thought filled Nick with dread. He actually didn't want to finish yet. *"Jah,"* he said reluctantly. "Unless something goes wrong." The truth was, if he worked all afternoon on Saturday, he'd be done by evening. He didn't tell Lucy that, though. "Speaking of finishing, I think I've had it for the night, what about you? The fire is nearly out."

"Jah, my eyes are going to cross if I work on this any longer."

"I heard there's a gathering after the singing. Would you like to stop by? Maybe we ought to reinforce the idea we're a couple."

Lucy pulled her head back and looked at him wide-eyed. Uh-oh, did she think he meant they ought to convince their peers by kissing each other again? "I mean, they'll see us together again."

"Oh, okay," she said hesitantly. "I suppose that would be all right."

She didn't seem enthusiastic about the offer, but now that he'd proposed it, Nick didn't know how to take it back. He suggested she remain inside until he loaded his things into the buggy and then he'd return to double-check that there were no live embers in the fireplace. But when he stepped outside, everything was dusted in a fine, fluffy powder and he had an idea.

"It snowed enough to sled down the hill in the back at least once," he told her. "If you think Penny is fast, you're going to love this!"

Lucy didn't question how he knew about the hill—she probably assumed he'd been sledding with his *Englisch* friend there before, but she did ask, "Do the Nelsons have a sled we can use?"

Nick hadn't thought of that, but he didn't let it stop him. "*Neh*, but we can use the lids to their garbage cans. Kevin and I used to do that all the time when we were *kinner*."

Lucy laughed. "Okay, if you go first."

Nick retrieved the two round metal tops to the garbage cans and flicked on the floodlight over the back deck. It illuminated a steep hill that disappeared into the darkness below. They made their way to the backyard, where Nick solemnly advised Lucy, "When you get to the bottom of the hill, if the sled—I mean the garbage can cover—doesn't stop, you need to roll off it. Otherwise you'll keep going right into the woods.

There's a little ditch at the very end of the slope, but after that, it's all trees. I don't want you crashing into one."

"This sounds risky."

"That's what makes it so thrilling," Nick teased, "Don't be a chicken, Luce."

"Who's a chicken?" she bantered. "Not me. I'll go first if you want me to."

Nick had no doubt she would have, but he wanted to be sure he was at the bottom of the hill when she came down in case he needed to help stop her. "No way, I'm going first. I already called it! Now give me a push."

He plunked himself down on the lid, crossed his legs into a pretzel shape and scooted himself toward the edge of the hill. Lucy placed her hands on his shoulders and pushed for all she was worth, running a few feet behind him until he picked up steam and was sailing through the dark. The snow was so scant he figured most of his speed was gained from sliding over old, wet leaves, but it hardly mattered—he was cruising. Within seconds he'd reached the end of the decline and since he was traveling too fast to stop, he rolled off the garbage can lid just in time. The metal lid continued its trajectory without him, rattling against the rocks in the gully at the base of the hill.

"Are you all right?" Lucy called.

"*Jah.* But I'm not so sure about the lid," he yelled back. "Maybe you shouldn't do this after all."

"Just try to stop me!" she taunted, and then all was quiet until he saw her flying over the crest of the hill. She squawked, "Ahh!"

Nick could tell she was too light to steer the lid in a forward motion; it was spinning around and around as she zoomed down the hill, completely out of control. "Roll!" he yelled as she approached the end. "Roll off, now!"

But she had gained too much momentum. She was tearing right toward the gully! Nick jumped in her path and his lower legs suffered most of the blow as she barreled into him. For someone so thin, she packed a punch, and he flipped over her head and landed on his side as she continued traveling—slowly but unstoppably— smack into the gully.

"Lucy!" he yelled even before he was upright. He'd never forgive himself if she was hurt. "Lucy! Lucy, answer me! Are you all right?"

Suddenly, he saw her head pop up in the ditch. "I'm fine. Are you okay?"

He didn't know if his knees were weak from relief or from being knocked into by her, but he fell onto his backside in the snow. "*Jah*, I am now," he uttered weakly.

"*Gut!*" she exclaimed. "Because I never did anything like that before, but I want to do it again!"

They managed to get in three more turns apiece until there was no discernible snow left to sled on. As they slowly hiked back up the hill together a final time, Lucy's breathing was heavy so Nick slowed his pace.

"That was such *schpass*," she gushed deliriously. "I didn't know I had it in me to do something like that!"

"Really?" Nick was surprised. "I never had any doubt," he said.

Chapter Nine

When Lucy awoke in the early hours of Saturday morning shivering with cold, she figured she had never completely warmed up after sledding with Nick. She rose and donned a pair of wool socks, added another quilt to her bed and then drifted back to sleep. But when she woke again at sunrise and had a coughing fit that rivaled the performance she'd put on for Mrs. Nelson, she knew she wasn't just cold. She was sick.

She intended to hide her condition from Betty and her father, but they noticed the moment she finally walked into the kitchen sometime later, while everyone else was eating breakfast.

"What happened to you?" Mildred asked. "You look *baremlich.*"

"I just overslept," Lucy began to say, but she interrupted herself coughing.

Her father immediately rose from his chair and placed his hand on her forehead. He'd been the one checking her for fever since she was a child, and the weight of his hand on her head was so familiar it was comforting even if she was sick.

"You're running a fever. You need to go back to bed."

"Here, let me feel her," Betty said, and took a turn placing her hand over Lucy's forehead. "Ach, he's right. You are a little warm. I'll make some tea and bring it to you upstairs. Katura, go fill the hot water bottle for Lucy. Mildred, please see to it she has enough pillows. She should keep her head elevated so she doesn't cough."

Lucy wanted to argue, but she acknowledged another hour of sleep would do her good. After that she'd be refreshed and ready to get to work on her weekend chores and then her embroidery orders. Climbing the stairs, she felt like she had lead in her socks. Mildred helped put a fresh case on a second pillow while Lucy removed a third quilt from the shelf in the closet.

Then Katura entered the room. "Have you seen the hot water bottle?" she asked.

Lucy gestured toward the chest of drawers. "It's in there, I think." She eased herself into bed as Katura pulled a drawer open.

"Look at this!" she exclaimed, and pulled out the box of candy from Nick that Lucy had hidden there. Katura lifted the lid and looked inside. "No wonder you're sick. How long have you had this? It's half gone."

"That's mine," Lucy said, and Katura dropped it back into the drawer.

"I know it's yours. I wasn't going to take it, but you don't have to be so selfish." She flounced out of the room without locating the hot water bottle.

Lucy hadn't meant Katura couldn't have any candy; she'd responded only like that because she was surprised her stepsister had opened her private gift from

Nick without asking first. "I didn't mean to offend Katura," she mumbled. Her lips and throat were dry and she felt teary. "You can both have some if you want."

"Denki." Mildred didn't hesitate to retrieve the box from the drawer. Even though it wasn't yet nine o'clock in the morning, she helped herself to a big piece of peanut brittle. "Yum, this is the expensive stuff. Did you get it from Nick?"

Lucy nodded, smiling at the memory. She felt so sick she didn't mind if Mildred ate the rest of the candy, but Lucy was going to save the box as a cherished memento.

"I can't wait until I have a suitor who brings me gifts like this," Mildred said in between bites, and Lucy smiled. Nick might not have been her suitor, but that didn't mean the gift wasn't thoughtful all the same. Uncharacteristically empathetic, Mildred said, "Don't pay any attention to Katura. Her nose is bent out of shape because Frederick Stutzman gave Fern Slagel a ride home from the caroling practice last night."

"Really? Fredrick and Fern?" Lucy was glad to know he was pursuing another courtship. Or that his mother was pursuing it for him. "But why would Katura be upset about that?"

Mildred rummaged through the box for another piece of peanut brittle. "She's developed a little crush on Frederick, but don't let on like you know. That's why she's so upset about Nick being your suitor. First you turned down Frederick and now Nick is courting you. She feels like she should be courting someone first, since she's older than you are."

"Only by three months," Lucy said drowsily, and she wondered if she was dreaming. Because Katura made no attempt to hide her interest in Nick, it was surreal to discover she was interested in Frederick. Aloud Lucy muttered, "There's nothing to be envious of. Nick isn't really courting me."

"What?" Mildred's ears perked up, but Lucy was too tired to fix her mistake.

And then Betty must have walked in with a cup of tea. Lucy couldn't lift her eyelids to look, but she could faintly smell the honey-lemon tea—which actually contained no tea, just honey, lemon and hot water—Betty served whenever someone had a cold.

"I think she dozed," Mildred told her mother. "But she's definitely feverish. She was just talking gibberish about Nick."

"Is that candy you're eating? At this hour?" Lucy heard Betty ask Mildred. That was the last thing she remembered before falling asleep.

Even though he had told his father he wanted to spend the afternoon with Lucy on Saturday, Nick worked at the hardware store until closing time because he decided he'd rather stall his project than to forfeit an excuse to go out with Lucy the following week. So when she didn't come to the porch a few minutes after six thirty, their agreed-upon time, Nick decided to take the opportunity to greet Betty and Marvin. He climbed the steps and had lifted his hand to knock on the door when Katura emerged.

"Hello, Nick," she said warmly. "It's *gut* to see you, but Lucy's been sick all day, so she can't go out with you."

Nick's heart tripped, missing a beat. "She's been sick? How sick?"

Katura rolled her eyes. "It's probably just a case of the sniffles, but with Lucy, everyone babies her if she so much as sneezes. Anyway, where were the two of you going? There's a party after caroling practice, you know."

Nick had to think fast. Since he hadn't worked on the repairs that afternoon at all, he and Lucy had planned to spend a few hours at the cabin and then stop by the party after the rehearsal by way of putting in an appearance. Now that Lucy couldn't come with him, Nick figured he should briefly drop in on the carolers first and then go to the cabin. That way, even if his parents found out Lucy was sick, Nick could legitimately tell them he'd gone to the gathering instead of going out with her.

"*Jah*, I know. Since Lucy can't *kumme* out with me, I might drop by to listen to the carolers practice for a little while," he said.

"*Gut*, will you take me there, then?" Katura asked. "Since you're already here and all."

Nick stalled, trying to think of an excuse for not taking Katura without seeming rude. "I don't know how long I'll stay. If I leave before the rehearsal is over, you won't have a ride home."

"That's all right. By then Mildred will have arrived and she can bring me home. She's not ready to go to the singing just yet, but I'd like to get there early. I need all the practice I can get." Without waiting for Nick to agree to give her a ride, she added, "I'll go let her know I'm leaving now and I'll be right out."

Nick turned and waited in his buggy. He jiggled his knee, wondering what kind of illness Lucy had. If only he'd been able to talk to her for a few minutes…

"Can you help me up?" Katura asked when she arrived with a platter wrapped in tinfoil. "It's hard to balance this."

Instead of taking her hand, Nick reached for the platter. "You'll have an easier time if I take this for you." He placed the dish on the seat between them. "So, did Lucy ask you to give me a message or anything?" he inquired. He thought it was odd she didn't at least meet him at the door herself. If she was really that sick it must have struck quickly.

"She didn't say anything at all. Of course, she was sound asleep, so she couldn't have. Lucy's *daed* is the one who told me to tell you she couldn't go out tonight. But don't worry, he's just overly protective of her. I'm sure he doesn't blame you that she's ill."

Nick hadn't been worried until Katura mentioned that. It *was* kind of his fault—he was the one who'd suggested sledding. Nick swallowed, silently praying Lucy would recover after a bit of rest.

"Would you tell her I'm sorry she's under the weather?" Nick asked.

"I will if she's awake when I get home," Katura agreed. "You know what a little mouse she is. She always scurries off to a corner and hardly talks to anyone. And even if the only thing she does all day is sew, she's in bed by the time the clock strikes nine. Now that she's sick, she'll probably be even more lethargic."

"That doesn't sound like the Lucy I know at all," Nick said, annoyed her stepsister was casting her in such a poor light. "She might be small but she's a ball of energy. And when she's quiet it's because unlike some people, she waits until she has something to say before she opens her mouth."

He hadn't directly been making a comparison between Lucy and Katura, but to young women like Katura. However, she was insulted, apparently, by his insinuation, because she folded her arms across her chest and didn't say another word until they arrived at their destination.

"You can go ahead in while I hitch the horse," Nick suggested. The last thing he needed was for someone to start a rumor because they arrived together.

Katura stuck out her lower lip as Nick handed her the platter, and then she stamped across the yard toward the big barn where tonight's singing was being held. Now that he was here, Nick realized how hungry he was. He didn't want to sing, but he could at least grab some food before going to Jenny's house.

To his surprise, when he crossed the threshold he noticed several *Englisch* young people mingling with the Amish. Nick made his way to the snack table where Kevin was stacking cookies onto a plate. "What's going on? Why are the *Englisch* here?" he asked his brother.

"Our carolers invited some of the *Englisch* churches' singles' groups to go with them this year. They've been rehearsing separately, but since they'll be singing together all week in public when they begin making their caroling rounds tomorrow evening, they wanted to squeeze in a practice session tonight."

"*Jah*, well, don't forget what happened the last time you were around the *Englisch*," Nick warned. He recognized a few of the *Englisch* youth and he was surprised they were here. They didn't seem like the type who'd be interested in singing. Maybe Nick was misjudging them, but he was going to have to keep an eye on Kevin.

"Nick, try one of these." Katura interrupted his thoughts, elbowing Nick in the side and holding out a gingerbread cookie. Kevin took the opportunity to leave, presumably before Nick could lecture him any further.

"It's *appenditlich*," he mumbled after biting into it. It was actually too crunchy for his taste, but Nick didn't want to stay on Katura's bad side, especially since he was relying on her to pass his message along to Lucy.

"Hi there, stranger," a female said, tapping him on the shoulder. Nick twisted around to see Jenny Nelson.

"Hi, Jenny," he replied awkwardly, unnerved by the possibility she might mention the cabin repairs in front of Katura. After introducing the two women, Nick said, "I didn't know you like to sing, Jenny."

"I don't, but I just missed you at the hardware store today. Kevin told me I might find you here tonight. Since I really needed to talk to you about—"

"I don't sing, either," Nick cut her off. "And it sounds like they're about to start, so why don't we go outside to talk? Excuse us, Katura."

Katura's eyebrows were raised. "Of course, you two go chat in private," she remarked pointedly, causing Nick to worry about what she might be assuming.

Outside he said to Jenny, "Sorry for interrupting you like that, but no one knows about the cabin repairs. I didn't want Katura finding out."

"Don't worry, I wasn't going to say anything explicit. I've kept it a guarded secret, too. But I wanted to hear about your progress. My mother's been considering taking Monday afternoon off work to get a head start on cleaning the cabin."

Nick panicked. "Monday? I thought I had until Wednesday or even Thursday!"

"There's no chance you can complete the work early?"

"*Neh.* That would mean I'd have to finish it tonight since I can't work on the Sabbath." Even if Nick worked until midnight as fast as he could, he still wouldn't be able to finish the project. What's more, he wasn't prepared to call off his arrangement with Lucy yet.

Jenny frowned. "I'd hoped if you had enough time to come here, it meant maybe you were further along with the project."

"I can understand why you'd think that," Nick admitted. "But even if I had skipped the party, there's no way I could have finished everything at the cabin tonight. I'll do as much as I can though. Maybe I can finish by Tuesday. And just so you know, I only stopped by here to grab something to eat. I'm on my way to your cabin now."

"Okay, I'll do my best to keep my mother from coming over early. She has a million things to do in preparation for Christmas anyway, so if she takes the afternoon off I'll suggest she goes shopping or something."

"*Denki,*" Nick said. "If you stop by the hardware store on Tuesday, I can update you on my progress then."

Jenny agreed, and then Nick said he had to get going. She replied, "Since you're going past my house, can I have a ride home? My friends are going to be here all night. And I've never ridden in a buggy in the winter before."

Nick couldn't say no after Jenny had been so patient about his progress on the cabin. "Sure," he agreed.

Jenny dashed inside to let her friends know she had a ride home. "All set?" Nick asked when she hoisted herself into the seat next to him.

"Yeah. They were in the middle of a song so I didn't want to interrupt them, but your friend Katura said she'd pass along the message for me."

Terrific, that's all I need—Katura starting a rumor about Jenny and me. But Nick had more pressing concerns on his mind. Namely, he was worried about Lucy. After Nick dropped Jenny at the end of her driveway, he continued to the cabin. He'd worked by himself there every night except Friday, but suddenly the place seemed to echo with emptiness because Lucy wasn't there. A month ago, Nick could have gone for an entire year without so much as waving hello to her; now, he missed her after spending even a single day apart. The longing felt nearly unbearable, so as Nick worked, he again prayed for Lucy's healing, adding, *And Lord, please give me patience until I can see her again.*

Lucy's head was swimming as she slowly made her way downstairs. Even before she reached the kitchen, she could smell something cooking and she felt guilty she'd slept so long; she had planned to make shepherd's pie for lunch, but Betty must have made something else instead.

When Betty saw Lucy, she set down a pot and came to Lucy's side. "How are you feeling?" she asked. Lucy saw the concern in her eyes. Betty wasn't her mother, but she had undeniable maternal instincts toward Lucy.

"A little groggy but much better. Sorry I overslept," she said. Katura and Mildred were clearing the table.

"I was planning to make shepherd's pie, but it looks like you've already eaten lunch."

"Lunch?" Betty's forehead wrinkled. "We're cleaning up after breakfast."

"You are? But you just ate breakfast. What time is it?"

"It's eight o'clock in the morning. Sunday morning. You slept right through lunch and supper yesterday. Through the night, too," Mildred announced.

"Really?" Lucy was utterly discombobulated.

"It's true," Betty said, lifting her hand to Lucy's forehead. "Your fever is gone but you're very pale. Go sit in the parlor, and I'll fix you a cup of tea. Katura, please check to see if the fire needs more logs."

While Katura stoked the fire in the woodstove, Lucy took a seat next to it. *If I slept all through Saturday, what happened when Nick showed up yesterday evening?* she wondered. Katura seemed to read her mind.

"Don't worry, last night when Nick showed up I told him you were sick and couldn't go out. But he was kind enough to give me a ride to caroling practice. Penny is every bit as fast as I've heard she is."

Lucy was immediately ruffled. Did Nick take as much pleasure in demonstrating to Katura how fast Penny could run as when he'd shown Lucy? She brooded over why he had taken Katura to the rehearsal anyway. He had work to do on the cabin, so why was he at the practice? Then Lucy realized that since she'd been sick, Nick probably didn't have an excuse to get out of going to the rehearsal. She was dismayed to realize her illness had probably hindered his work.

Katura blathered on, "Of course, I had to ride home with Mildred since Nick left early with an *Englischer*.

She was a blonde woman, but what was her name?" Katura tapped her chin as if trying to remember. "Ah, right, it was Jenny. Jenny Nelson. She was one of the *Englisch* carolers who came to the rehearsal, but she said she didn't like to sing. She'd *kumme* there looking for Nick. The two of them took off together after about ten minutes."

Lucy felt queasy. *Jenny* Nelson? Nick's friend whose family owned the cabin was a woman? Lucy had assumed his friend was a man, an assumption Nick allowed her to believe by not correcting her when she referred to him as the Nelson boy. Come to think of it, Nick hadn't ever told her his friend's name, had he? Why would he have concealed the fact his friend was a female? Lucy could think of only one reason. Suddenly, she felt like her lungs were made of cement and each breath she took required enormous effort.

Nick couldn't possibly be romantically interested in Jenny. Although Nick hadn't been baptized yet and technically could date an *Englischer*, Lucy had no doubt he was true to his faith. He was true to the Amish. But was he true to Lucy? *Did he set me up from the beginning?* she speculated. *Or am I letting my imagination run away with me because I feel so crummy?*

Lucy struggled to contain her qualms. Her trembling hands didn't go unnoticed when Betty brought her another cup of lemon tea.

"Steady now, or you'll spill it." Lucy's stepmother hovered over her, clucking her tongue. "It's a *gut* thing it's an off Sunday—you need more rest today."

Lucy swallowed a sip of the hot liquid before protesting. "I feel much better now, and by evening, I'll have even more energy. All that sleep really helped."

She felt desperate to see Nick so she could address the situation between him and Jenny.

"I'm glad you're feeling better, but you still need to stay in today. No visitors," Betty said authoritatively, which annoyed Lucy. She wasn't a child.

When her father came in from outdoors carrying wood in his arms, Lucy told him how much better she felt, assuming he'd side with her about going out with Nick that evening. Instead, he deliberately arranged a log in the fire and said, "You're an adult, Lucy, so I'm not going to stop you from going out. But I think you should exercise common sense and do what's right for your health. I also think anyone who truly cares about you would be willing to wait another day or two until you're more rested before taking you out in the cold."

Her father's reference to Nick wasn't lost on Lucy, and since she didn't want him to think poorly of Nick, she begrudgingly agreed she'd stay in and wouldn't receive visitors. Besides, it was the Sabbath so it wasn't as if Nick could work on the cabin anyway. Even though she was desperate to see him for her own sake, Lucy was relieved her absence wouldn't set him back on the cabin repairs. Still, she harbored hope he'd stop by the house. That way, maybe she could settle her qualms by asking him about Jenny Nelson.

But the hours ticked by and there was no sign of Nick. While he wasn't obligated to check on her, Lucy was surprised he didn't, especially since the other night he'd claimed how concerned he was about her health. She tried to convince herself he didn't want to bother her while she was recovering, but her thoughts kept circling back to Jenny Nelson. Why hadn't he mentioned his friendship with her if indeed there was nothing to hide?

Fidgety all day, Lucy was too listless to work on embroidering her final napkin for the auction and by the time Katura and Mildred left for rehearsal, Lucy was grumpier than ever. It just figured the one time she actually wouldn't mind chaperoning them, Lucy was forbidden to go.

While Lucy silently stewed in the corner of the parlor, Betty brought her a piece of mail. "This came for you yesterday," she said. "I forgot all about it."

The return address indicated it was from Bridget so Lucy retreated to her room to read it. She carefully unsealed the gold envelope to reveal a homemade Christmas card. On the front Bridget had designed a simple star sparkling with glitter. Above it were the words, "All is bright," in big print. Beneath the star she'd inscribed the King James Version of John 8:12: "Then spake Jesus again unto them, saying, I am the light of the world: he that followeth me shall not walk in darkness, but shall have the light of life."

The note inside was short but sweet:

Dear Lucy,
Thank you for your beautiful card. I won't forget my skates and I'll also pack an extra pair of leggings to cushion me when I inevitably fall on my backside!

Even though I'll see you in a week, I have to tell you something that can't wait that long, something I can only confide in you about... I have a suitor. His name is Joshua and he's a mason. I've never met anyone like him. He's dependable and trustworthy, not to mention good-natured and strong. One look from him and I forget my own name. I think I'm in love.

I can't wait to see you!
Love from your cousin,
Bridget

Sliding the card back into its envelope, Lucy suddenly understood how Katura felt—or at least, how Mildred said Katura felt—because Lucy had a suitor and Katura didn't. Even though Lucy loved Bridget like a sister, she had to admit she was envious. Lucy wanted good things for her cousin, but she wanted them for herself, too. *I want to be able to claim* I'm *in love and I want it to be real*, she lamented. She was tired of playing at a courtship and she was disheartened to realize Nick wasn't as "dependable and trustworthy" as Bridget claimed her Joshua was.

The worst part was, Lucy couldn't even confront Nick about his relationship with Jenny because Lucy was housebound. She was sick. Fragile. Weak. If Lucy was so frail she couldn't go out on a Sunday evening like everyone else her age, how had she fooled herself into thinking she might have been on her way to falling in love? How had she dared hope someone might fall in love with her, might wish to marry her?

It serves me right, she thought. *I tried so hard to convince others Nick and I were courting I almost wound up believing it myself.*

If there was one good thing about being ill it was that she had no energy left over to do anything else, including cry. So, instead, Lucy layered her bed with as many quilts as she could gather and dropped into a deep sleep.

* * *

Nick had a list of reasons for being agitated. Not only had he missed seeing Lucy on Saturday night, but he had stayed awake until two o'clock waiting for Kevin to return home. Nick met him at the door demanding to know why he was out so late. In response, Kevin lipped off, saying he didn't need a lecture from Nick.

"Better from me than from *Daed*," Nick had retorted. After all he'd sacrificed to repair the cabin—including indirectly putting Lucy's health at risk—his brother didn't seem to care one whit. Nick was beginning to wonder if he should have just allowed Kevin to suffer the consequences of his actions.

Then, on Sunday afternoon, Nick had intended to take a ride to visit Lucy, but his aunt and uncle and their family stayed later than they expected and once again Nick was corralled into entertaining his younger cousins. It was seven o'clock before Nick could finally break away. He wasn't sure what to do—stop at Lucy's or go to the singing in hopes of seeing her there. He was concerned if he stopped at her house and Lucy was still ill Katura would rope him into giving her a ride again. Ultimately, he decided he'd go to the singing first and find out if Lucy was feeling better. If not, he'd pay her a visit at home.

When he arrived, he didn't see her near the snack table, nor did he find her in the parlor. Aware she had a penchant for withdrawing to a quiet place, he looked but didn't find her in the bedroom where the coats were piled, either. Nick would have to ask one of her stepsisters where she was. When he spied Katura whispering into Melinda's ear, he circumvented the pair and located Mildred in the kitchen instead.

"*Jah*, she feels a lot better, but her *daed* strongly suggested she stay in," Mildred said. She'd just finished eating a cupcake and was licking frosting from her fingers.

"Okay. I'll pay her a visit at home, then," Nick replied, starting for the door.

"Uh, I wouldn't do that if I were you."

Nick did a double take. Was Lucy angry he hadn't checked in on her health? "Why not?"

"Her *daed* said something to the effect of anyone who really cared about her would give her time to get better. I'm pretty sure he was talking about you."

"Oh." Nick pulled his ear. He supposed that made sense. But how long would he have to wait? Then he was struck with an idea. "Could you give her a note from me?"

"Sure," Mildred agreed. Then she tittered, "I've never delivered a *liebesbrief* before."

Nick was too distracted trying to find a pen and piece of paper to reply to Mildred's remark. He found a felt-tipped pen someone had left near a list of the songs they were practicing, but all he had to write on was a napkin. Since there was no way to keep his comments private he kept them short.

Dear Lucy,
I'm sorry you've been ill. I hope it's all right if I call on you tomorrow night at six. Maybe if you're feeling better I can take you out for supper?
Nick

The ink was bleeding into the napkin, distorting his already messy penmanship, but it would have to do. He folded it in half. "Please don't lose this," Nick urged Mildred.

"I won't use it," she answered, having misheard him over the singing, which had begun in the next room. Then she added, "I won't read it, either."

Nick didn't care one way or another if she did, as long as she delivered it to Lucy. Since there was no longer any reason to stay at the singing, he headed for home as fast as Penny could take him. All he wanted was to go to sleep and wake up one day closer to seeing Lucy again.

Chapter Ten

Nick wants to take me out for supper? Lucy could only imagine it was because he felt guilty about Katura catching him sneaking off with Jenny. Lucy would go with him, but only to tell him she was ending their arrangement. She decided since she was finishing the last of the linen napkins anyway it would be better if she didn't prolong the inevitable by continuing to walk out with Nick even one more day. She was going to confront him about Jenny, too. Not that Lucy needed an explanation at this point, but she was curious. Also, she wanted to watch him squirm when he discovered Lucy knew about his relationship with an *Englischer*.

As eager as she was to end her arrangement with Nick, Lucy dreaded telling her stepsisters and Betty she was no longer being courted by him. It would only be a matter of time before Melinda Schrock found out, too, and she'd humiliate Lucy with her smug I-told-you-so comments. It wasn't as if Lucy would be in poor company; plenty of young women had been ditched by Nick. In this case, at least Lucy had the satisfaction of being the one who was doing the ditching. Besides, Bridget was coming soon. She'd console Lucy. *Either that, or she'll tell me I shouldn't have been so foolish in the first place since I knew what Nick did to her.*

"Are you sure you're up to going out tonight?" Betty fretted. Lucy was glad her father was working late so he wasn't home to add to the anxiety.

"*Jah.* I'm only going out for supper. I shouldn't be gone for more than an hour or two."

"I hope not," her stepmother said. "Your father and I have been lenient about you going out on weeknights because… Well, I'm beginning to have second thoughts about our decision."

Out of respect for her father and Betty, Lucy carefully considered their advice and concerns, but that didn't mean Lucy needed their permission to go out at night. Once again, she resented Betty treating her like a child. Worse, Lucy suspected her stepmother had been close to saying they'd been lenient about allowing Lucy to go out during the week because they figured it was so rare for her to be courted they'd better take advantage of it while the taking was good. Even if their assessment was right, it was hurtful.

"I know the limitations of my health," Lucy retorted with needles in her voice. She rebelled by waiting on the porch for fifteen minutes before Nick was scheduled to arrive. By the time his buggy circled the bend, her nose was so cold she couldn't feel it.

"Lucy!" Nick exclaimed when he saw her. "You shouldn't have waited outside for me. You're shivering."

"I'm aware," she said, her voice even frostier than her face.

Nick tipped his head curiously. "Here, let me help you up."

"I can manage," Lucy said, pushing his hand away. Since she hadn't bothered to bring her embroidery, she used both hands to pull herself into the buggy. She allowed Nick to arrange the blanket around her, but even that irritated her. It was as if he were tucking a baby into its cradle.

They were barely down the lane when Nick said, "It's so *gut* to see you again. I was worried when I heard you were sick."

"I was hardly sick," Lucy scoffed. "I barely even had a cold. I just needed rest."

"Still, I thought maybe you'd gotten ill from playing around in the snow like we did."

"*Neh.* It wasn't your fault, if that's what you're worried about."

Nick pulled his spine up straight. "I wasn't concerned because I felt guilty. I mean I did feel guilty, but my primary concern was for you, Lucy."

Lucy wouldn't give an inch. "Well, you can see I'm fine now," she snapped.

Nick slowed the horse and turned to look at her. "I can see you're not sick, but you're definitely not fine. You're upset about something. What is it?"

Beneath the streetlamp Lucy noticed Nick's bushy eyebrows furrowed with puzzlement. It took all of her willpower to resist telling him to never mind, it didn't matter. But it did. "I think you know what it is."

Nick tipped his head to the side, completely baffled. "Was it because I didn't *kumme* to see you yesterday?" he asked. "I wanted to. But Mildred warned me your *daed* said you needed rest. I didn't want to upset anyone."

Lucy hadn't realized he'd wanted to see her on Sunday. That was sweet of him, but it didn't change the fact he'd left the singing with an *Englischer* on Saturday evening, the same *Englischer* he'd been pretending was a male friend. Sure Nick wanted to see Lucy on Sunday; he probably needed to secure their arrangement. He needed to make sure her illness wouldn't interfere with his Monday night plans to restore Jenny's cabin.

"You don't have an obligation to check on me when I'm sick," she said. "You're not my doctor."

"I know that, Lucy!" Nick barked, his eyes flashing. "But I do care about you. I thought you understood that."

"And *I* thought you were being honest with me," she shot back.

"Honest with you? I *am* being honest with you. I honestly don't know what I've done to offend you."

Lucy perceived he was genuinely perplexed, and suddenly she wondered if she'd made a mistaken assumption about his relationship with Jenny. After all, even if he didn't correct Lucy when she referred to his Nelson family friend as a male, he had never explicitly told her his friend was a male. And maybe Katura had misinterpreted the situation with him leaving the party. It wouldn't have been the first time her stepsister had spread a false rumor.

Still uncertain she should let him off the hook, Lucy pressed, "Are you sure there's nothing about our arrangement you haven't told me that you want to?"

Nick slouched and covered his face with his hands before letting them drop to his lap. "Okay. There is something I haven't been honest about. Something I didn't tell you because I was afraid of how you'd react," he said, and as he turned to face her, Lucy inhaled deeply, bracing herself for the truth.

* * *

Nick hesitated, knowing what he was about to say would change the course of their relationship. It might even put an immediate end to their arrangement. But in this moment, he didn't care about finishing the cabin repairs or even about his father's reaction to the situation. All he cared about was that Lucy knew how he felt about her. The urgency to share his innermost feelings with Lucy threatened to consume him if he didn't tell her now.

"I… Over the course of this arrangement…of getting to know you…" Nick's throat was scorching. He had to stop stammering and just say the words. "I've developed feelings for you, Lucy. Romantic feelings."

Lucy's eyes widened noticeably behind her lenses, but she remained silent. With his heart pummeling his ribs, Nick bumbled onward. "I haven't known what to make of them. Haven't known whether they were authentic or whether I got caught up in pretending to walk out with you. But the more I've gotten to know you, the more I've realized my feelings are real and I'd like our courtship to be real, too. If you feel the same way, that is."

He scrutinized Lucy's face, but her expression was impassive. Penny snorted and flicked her tail. Lucy was clearly dumbfounded, but whether that was because his admission pleased her or disturbed her he couldn't tell. Was she trying to think of a way to let him down gently? When she remained silent, Nick's hope wilted.

Just when he thought he couldn't endure her lack of response another instant, she cleared her throat. "So you're not romantically interested in someone else?"

Now Nick was nonplussed. "What? No, of course not. Who would I be—? No, there's no one else I'm interested in. Only you, Luce."

There was no mistaking the flush of pleasure blossoming across Lucy's face. "I feel the same way about you, Nick."

He all but shouted *"Wunderbaar!"* and enveloped her in a tight bear hug before giving her a big kiss on the cheek. She instantly pulled back and exclaimed, "Oh!" But then she nodded and leaned toward him again, so this time he kissed her slowly and sweetly, warming her lips with his.

"Does that mean you'll have me as your suitor?" he asked. "For real?"

"For real," she replied. Their third kiss was long and firm, unequivocally sealing their new arrangement.

After they sat back against their seats again, Nick asked, "So, uh, may I take you to supper now?"

"Please."

"Please may I take you to supper now?"

"Neh, I mean, please do," Lucy said with a giggle.

"Oh, right." Nick blushed. He'd never felt so fazed by a woman's kisses before. "Where would you like to go?"

"It doesn't matter as long as it's warm," Lucy replied, rubbing her palms together.

Nick slid closer to her and embraced her shoulders. She fit so snugly beneath his arm it felt as if they'd always traveled this way. "Hang on, we'll be there in no time," he said, and Penny took off as quickly as Nick allowed.

They went to Hank's Hideout, a popular pizza place for Amish and *Englisch* young people alike. Nick was disappointed when they didn't see anyone there they knew. He'd never really made a public spectacle of his courtships before, but with Lucy, he wanted people to know about it now that it was real.

"Everyone will probably stop here after caroling tonight," she said. Then she asked him about his progress on the cabin.

"I'm almost done," he said. "I've got to make a few finishing touches, clean up my supplies and air out the place so it looks as *gut* as new. How much do you have to finish on your project?"

"I'm almost done, too. I didn't even bring my supplies with me tonight. After we eat I can help you clean up at the cabin if you want."

Nick shook his head vehemently. He'd gotten enough done on Saturday evening after dropping Jenny off that he was confident he could tie up the loose ends in no time. "I can do that tomorrow night. Tonight, how about if we just enjoy being together since it's our first official night of walking out?"

"I'd like that. Besides, I told Betty I wouldn't be out for more than a couple hours. She's worried I'll get run-down again," Lucy admitted. "I just hope you don't catch whatever I had."

It was worth it, he thought. Fortunately, the server brought them their food right then, which Nick hoped kept Lucy from noticing his ears were burning.

"I see your illness didn't affect your appetite," he teased when she reached for her fourth piece of pizza.

"Hey! I didn't eat anything all day on Saturday and hardly anything yesterday, either. I'm making up for lost time."

That's what Nick felt like he was doing: making

up for lost time. All those years of courting weren't a waste, but they didn't compare to being Lucy's suitor. Usually he felt pressured to spend more time than he wanted to with the women he was courting, but with Lucy, he felt he couldn't spend *enough* time with her. He was already looking forward to seeing Lucy again on Wednesday, when he would accompany her to the soup kitchen.

"Are you sure you don't want to go somewhere else this evening?" he pleaded after paying the bill.

"I do, but I'd better keep my word to Betty," she said. "Let's take the long way, though, so we can see the lights in town."

Lucy's countenance was as luminous as the landscape as they traveled toward her home. The *Englisch* residents of Willow Creek decorated their homes and yards with bright lights, and the Amish placed candles in their windows and simple wreaths on their doors. The effect was mesmerizing, and the only thing that could have made it more festive was if it had been snowing again.

Nick noticed a lamp on at Lucy's home and he saw a shadow pass by the window, but he didn't care who might be peeking out; after helping Lucy down from the buggy, he held her gloved fingers in his hands. "One more kiss?" he asked.

"Please," she said. This time he knew it was meant as an agreement, not a scolding, and he drew her to him. She stood on her tiptoes and he bent his head toward hers.

After they separated, he squeezed her hands before releasing them, too dazed to say anything as he watched her disappear into the house.

* * *

Four. Nick had kissed her four times tonight! *And every one of those kisses was as real as...as the lips on my face!* As she sprawled across her bed that evening remembering the sensation, Lucy lightly traced her mouth with her finger, nearly dizzy with giddiness. When she had set out with him that evening, she never could have envisioned the evening ending the way it did. Although she didn't know how to account for Nick not telling her his Nelson friend was a female, it no longer mattered. Lucy was relieved she hadn't accused him of being romantically involved with Jenny Nelson—not only would she have made a fool of herself, but Nick never would have wanted to court her.

Nick Burkholder is my suitor, she mused, nearly bursting with the desire to confide this development in another person. But who could she tell that didn't already think they were a couple? Lucy was hesitant to write to Bridget, knowing how Nick had acted toward her cousin in the past. *But he's changed,* she thought. Surely, Bridget would understand that? Lucy wasn't positive. She decided it would be better to tell her cousin in person, so instead of writing a letter, Lucy used a piece of stationery to doodle Nick's name beside hers as she daydreamed about their next kiss. *It can't* kumme *quickly enough,* she thought just before sleep overtook her.

The next evening, Lucy hummed Christmas carols as she slid a cookie sheet from the oven. This was her third batch, some she'd take to the soup kitchen and the rest would be for their family's celebration.

"Am I allowed to have one of these?" her father asked, reaching for one.

"*Neh!*" Lucy yipped. "They're hot. You'll burn your tongue. I've set aside a plate of them for you here, *Daed.*"

Her father accepted the dish as Betty came into the room. "You shouldn't be eating those," she said. "You know what the doctor said about your blood sugar."

Marvin hung his head like a scolded puppy. "You worry too much about my health."

"Now you know how I feel when you and Betty worry about me, *Daed,*" Lucy teased.

"I *don't* worry," Betty protested. "But I am vigilant. There's a difference."

"It's all the same to me if it means I can't have a cookie," Marvin grumbled, wrapping his arms around his wife's waist and kissing her on the cheek. Maybe it was because she was in love herself, but Lucy enjoyed witnessing this display of their affection.

"Oh, all right, you big *bobbel,*" Betty relented. "You can have a cookie. But just remember, I comment about your health because I care. And that goes for you, too, Lucy."

"I know it does—and I know *Daed* only comments because he cares, too," Lucy admitted, suddenly seeing their concern in a new light. "*Daed,* when you're finished eating those, will you please bring in the pine boughs?"

Her father had cut down evergreen branches from the trees near the back of their property so Lucy could make two wreaths—one for their door and one for the door in the church hallway leading to the soup kitchen. She savored the natural pine scent—one of the few fragrances that didn't cause her to cough or catch her breath—as she and her father twisted the branches into a circle and then tied them around a wire. Then Lucy affixed pine cones around the periphery of the wreath and fastened a crimson bow at the top. Her father declared their creation perfect, which was the same way Lucy felt about the evening itself.

She was cleaning up the materials when Mildred returned from caroling, her cheeks rosy.

"Where's Katura?" Lucy asked.

"She's riding home with…someone else," Mildred answered evasively, probably embarrassed to mention it in front of Lucy's father.

Lucy raised her eyebrows and mouthed, *Frederick?* to which Mildred nodded vigorously. A smile broke out over Lucy's face. It was easy to be happy for someone else when she was this happy herself, and she offered to serve everyone eggnog.

"That would be lovely," Betty agreed, looking pleased. Lucy always thought her stepmother placed too much emphasis on courtship, as if having a suitor was an accomplishment instead of a relationship. But now she realized Betty was as delighted that Katura had a suitor as she'd been that Lucy had one. And it wasn't necessarily because Betty was afraid the young women might never be courted, nor was it because Betty herself valued courtship so highly. It was because Betty was happy that her daughters—including Lucy—were happy.

The foursome chatted and ate and laughed until almost ten o'clock. Everyone was so jovial Lucy would have been reluctant to turn in for the night if it wasn't that she couldn't wait for Wednesday to arrive. Not only would she see Nick again, but the soup kitchen was hosting one big, final festive supper before Christmas. Lucy lay awake in bed anticipating the celebration long after Mildred's breathing vibrated in the steady rhythm of a snore. A few minutes before midnight, Katura crept into the room.

Lucy was quiet as her stepsister prepared to go to sleep, and when she heard Katura's bed creak as she positioned herself beneath her quilt, Lucy whispered, "Did you have a *gut* evening, Katura?"

She could see the faint outline of Katura's head pop up from her pillow, and then she tiptoed over to Lucy's bedside and knelt down so their faces were even. "*Jah.* Frederick gave me a ride home. He asked if he could court me and I said *jah!*"

"Oh, Katura, that's *wunderbaar!*" Lucy sat up and squeezed Katura's hand. "I'm really happy for you."

"*Denki,* but I don't know how you can be, Lucy. I've been wretched to you and I'm so sorry for the mean things I said." There was a pause before Katura continued, "I'm afraid I was jealous because you're younger than I am and you had a suitor first."

Recalling how she'd begrudged Bridget a suitor when Lucy didn't have one herself, she said, "I understand. I've experienced my share of jealousy, too. Though I have to say, I had no idea you were interested in Frederick."

"At first I wasn't. Or actually, I was but I didn't think he'd ever want to court me because I'm half a head taller than he is. I think that's why I was so envious of you. You're fortunate you're so short—you never have to consider whether you're too tall for a man to be confident enough to walk out with you."

"Ha!" Lucy sputtered. "I've never considered myself fortunate to be this short, but I accept that this is how *Gott* created me. Besides, I don't think height really matters to a man of character. Obviously, it doesn't matter to Frederick."

"*Neh*, it doesn't. Although I think he had to stand on tiptoes to kiss me," Katura said, giggling. In true fashion, she divulged more intimate details about her romantic relationship than Lucy would have shared. She added, "There's only one thing I'm worried about…"

"What's that?"

"His *mamm*. She's kind of, well, pushy. I'm pretty sure she's going to announce it to everyone that Frederick is courting me."

Lucy intended no offense when she said, "I'm surprised you mind if everyone knows."

"I don't," Katura said. "I just want the pleasure of announcing it myself."

Lucy laughed and Katura joined her until Mildred complained, "Would the two of you kindly stop discussing your courtships in front of me? My dreams are probably the only place I'll ever have a suitor, so I'd like to go back to sleep now, if that's okay with you."

"I doubt that's true, Mildred," Lucy replied. "But we'll be quiet now." She wanted to get to sleep as much as Mildred did so she'd be that much closer to seeing Nick.

But the next afternoon when she returned from work, Mildred presented Lucy a note Nick had brought to her at the mercantile. This time it wasn't a napkin; it was a folded piece of paper he had taped shut.

Dear Luce, *(funny how that nickname had grown on her)*
I am so sorry—*Lucy held her breath in trepidation; she knew yesterday was too good to be*

true—but I can't bring you to the soup kitchen tonight. I'll explain everything later. I still want to come and help serve, but I know you need to arrive early to set up, so it's better if your father takes you.

But I'd like to take you home. Let's go back the long way, okay?

Nick

Lucy remembered to exhale again. For a terrible moment, she thought Nick was going to call off their courtship. While she was disappointed he couldn't bring her to the soup kitchen, his reference to taking the long way home made her skin tingle. It was proof he wanted to be with her alone after their work at the soup kitchen was finished. What had she been so worried about?

Lucy's father said he was glad for the opportunity to spend time alone with her, but he asked if she'd mind if they stopped at the *Englisch* pottery shop on the way. "I'm picking up a gift I special ordered for Betty," he whispered. "The shop closes at five so I won't have time after I drop you off. I'll dash in and *kumme* right back out."

Tickled by her father's delight in buying a gift for his wife, Lucy thought, *I suppose it took being in love myself to appreciate it in others*, as she waited in the buggy. Cars and buggies streamed in and out of the parking lot in front of the small cluster of *Englisch* specialty shops. Lucy was trying to imagine what kinds of gifts the drivers intended to purchase when she spotted an Amish man with red curls sticking out from beneath his hat hitching his horse to the post. How many young redheaded Amish men were there in Willow Creek? Lucy only knew two: Nick and Kevin. *I must just have Nick on my mind*, she thought, giggling to herself. But when the man turned sideways, Lucy recognized it was definitely him. Why was Nick there instead of transporting her to the soup kitchen? Lucy's pulse ricocheted in her ears until she figured perhaps he had a special gift to pick up for his *mamm. Or maybe even for me*, she dared presume.

Her momentary calm was shattered an instant later when he strode not toward the store, but toward a car, where a young *Englisch* woman with long blond hair got out. Katura said Jenny Nelson was blond; who else could it be? Standing face-to-face the pair appeared to speak briefly before Nick took Jenny's hand. What Jenny did next sickened Lucy: she threw her arms around Nick in a big, delighted hug.

Her stomach cramping with revulsion, Lucy couldn't bear to watch any longer. She buried her face in her hands as her thoughts spiraled and her breath came in tight, short puffs. So she'd been right all along. Nick *was* engaged in a romantic relationship with Jenny Nelson. He must have sensed Lucy was on the brink of confronting him on Monday night. That's why he'd kissed her; he felt he had to pull out all the stops to distract Lucy from pressing the matter and exposing his secret romance with an *Englischer*. She never felt so used and betrayed in her life, and at that moment the very act of breathing in and out was more laborious than when she'd been hospitalized with pneumonia.

"Are you all right?" her father asked when he boarded the buggy. By then she was no longer gasping. Dropping her hands from her eyes, she looked up;

Nick's buggy was still there, but the *Englisch* car was gone. Wherever they went and whether they went together or alone, Lucy didn't care as they were out of her sight and out of her life.

Nick was relieved. Having completed the final touches on the repairs and cleaned up the cabin on Tuesday night, he had just handed the key over to Jenny and he was home free. From now on, he could dedicate every evening he went out to actually being with Lucy. Whistling, he entered the china shop, which was located between the pottery shop and the cutlery store. His frequent sensation of being a bull in a china shop around Lucy had given him an idea about what to get her for Christmas, which was why, when Jenny checked in with him at the hardware store on Tuesday, he'd asked her to meet him at this particular location today.

He searched the mirrored shelves in the store until at last he found exactly what he wanted: a white teacup and saucer decorated with a delicate, thin line of gold around the rims. The china was every bit as understatedly elegant as Lucy was to him. Assuring Nick the piece was sturdier than it looked, the clerk boxed it up in a nest of packing material. Nick stowed it beneath the seat of his buggy and then made haste to the soup kitchen.

When he arrived, Lucy hardly looked up from where she was arranging cookies on platters. At first Nick assumed she didn't see him, but when he said hello, she mumbled hello back and retreated to the kitchen without making eye contact. Was she miffed he hadn't picked her up? Nick didn't know, but he decided to follow her to find out.

Just as he reached the kitchen door she emerged carrying a wreath, and Dan followed close behind with a stepladder. Nick stood motionless, watching from a distance as Dan climbed the stepladder and pounded a nail into the wall above the door frame. Then Lucy handed him the wreath, which he hung. Clearly she thought it was crooked, because she motioned for him to step down so she could climb up and adjust it. She had to stand on tiptoe, and when the bow was precisely aligned, Lucy began to wobble. Dan lunged forward dramatically, swooped her into his arms and set her upright on the floor.

Seething, Nick dug his fingernails into his palms. He'd witnessed Lucy's rock-solid balance as she stood in his buggy at full speed, and he'd watched her glide on one foot across the rink at Wheeler's Pond without wavering. Her fall from the stepladder was contrived, undoubtedly to capture Dan's attention. Maybe that was why she was so indifferent to Nick's presence; maybe she liked Dan. But then why had she allowed Nick to kiss her only two days ago? Why had she agreed to accept him as her suitor? Nick recalled suddenly that Dan had seen Nick and Lucy's fake kiss at the singing. Nick remembered he had suspected Lucy was trying to make Dan jealous way back then. His mind was racing. Maybe accepting Nick as her suitor for real allowed Lucy to continue her ploy to win Dan over. Perhaps she felt that once her phony courtship with Nick ended, she wouldn't have any leverage to make Dan more interested in her.

Livid, Nick stalked across the room and cupped Lucy's elbow. "I need to speak with you, now," he said, escorting her down the hallway before she had a chance to protest.

He directed her to an empty room that must have been used as a nursery because there were animals painted on the walls and three cribs lined up in the far corner. Nick could practically feel steam escaping his nostrils as he fumed, "Just what is going on, Lucy?"

She yanked her arm free of his grasp and shoved her hands on her hips. "You tell me!"

Once again, Nick didn't know what she was talking about and it infuriated him. Instead of addressing any potential wrongdoing on his part, he said, "From what I can tell, you're flirting with Dan. Which is entirely your business, but if he's the one you're interested in, you should have had the decency to turn down my offer of courtship!"

"You want to talk about decency?" Lucy challenged, her voice rising. "Then tell me why *you* lied about being interested in Jenny Nelson! And don't deny it. I saw you holding her hand and hugging her in the parking lot at Buckland Corner today."

How dare Lucy imply he was romantically involved with Jenny, especially after Nick had demonstrated in no uncertain terms how he felt about Lucy! Did she still really have that low of an opinion of him?

"I can't believe you'd think I'm interested in her, but you don't have any idea what you're talking about. And quite frankly it disgusts me that you'd think I'd do anything so revolting as kiss one woman while I'm secretly courting another." Nick nearly choked on the words. "If you weren't so judgmental, you'd realize things aren't always as they seem to be, Lucy."

"*Neh?* Because what it *seems* like to me is you went to great lengths to keep it a secret that your Nelson friend was a woman. For all I know, you fabricated the entire situation with her cabin so you could use me as a cover for seeing her!"

"That's *lecherich* and you know it." Frustrated by Lucy's reasoning, Nick pounded a fist into his open palm as he snarled, "You saw me making the repairs yourself!"

Momentarily quiet, Lucy blinked repeatedly. It seemed she was backing down, but then she said, "Okay, Nick. I could be wrong. If you can look me in the eye and tell me you honestly were solely repairing the Nelsons' cabin out of the goodness of your heart… If you can tell me you simply wanted to give them a joyful *Grischtdaag* and that's all there is to it, I'll believe you. I'll apologize for ever doubting whether you've been completely truthful with me."

Nick swallowed, his head thrumming. He couldn't confirm what Lucy wanted him to confirm because it wasn't entirely true. But neither could he explain because then she'd be angry he hadn't been honest with her from the beginning. When his silence lengthened, Lucy threw her hands in the air and then slapped them against her sides. "Exactly as I thought." She spun on her heel and was gone before he could utter another syllable.

Suddenly, he didn't want to explain because he had nothing more to say to her. He didn't care if he never saw her again. He'd *prefer* it that way. Nick was so heated he didn't remember making his way to the buggy, and when Penny accelerated to a rapid canter on the way home, Nick derived no pleasure from the animal's agility or relief from the frigid air against his stinging cheeks.

By the next afternoon, Nick's anger had fizzled to a

sullen numbness, and he went through the motions of waiting on customers and wishing them holiday cheer although the words rung hollow. His ire was briefly ignited again when Betty Knepp entered the store and inquired after his mother's whereabouts.

"She's staying put at the house today. *Grischtdaag* baking and all that," Nick's father told her as Nick dallied within earshot in the fasteners aisle. "You should call on her. She'd *wilkom* an opportunity to take a break and have a cup of tea with you."

Nick's stomach flipped; he could guess why Betty Knepp would wish to call on his mother. Two days ago he wouldn't have dreamed Lucy would squeal on him, but two days might as well have been another lifetime. Everything had changed since then. Or everything had stayed the same: Lucy Knepp was still the same stuck-up, finger-pointing Goody Two-shoes she'd been as a child. Nick had no doubt he was going to get an earful from his parents that evening.

Indeed, after Nick closed shop and returned home, his parents were waiting for him in the parlor. He'd barely removed his boots and taken a seat by the fire when his mother bluntly inquired whether he was romantically involved with an *Englischer*.

Until that moment, he'd been holding out hope Lucy hadn't done exactly what he feared she'd done. Even when his mother questioned him, he still couldn't quite believe his ears. "Who told you that?" he asked, knowing full well it was Lucy.

"That's not important," his mother replied. "What's important is if it's true."

Nick looked directly into his mother's eyes. "*Neh*, I absolutely am not romantically involved with an

Englischer, and anyone who told you that is sorely mistaken," Nick asserted.

His mother's expression softened. "We believe you," she replied, and his father seconded her sentiment, nodding. "We know you've had a—er, a difficult time finding someone who was a *gut* match for you, but we doubted you'd ever court an *Englischer*. Especially while you were courting Lucy. The idea was unthinkable to us, but out of a sense of fairness, we wanted to confirm the truth with you before setting the wom— the person who started the rumor straight."

Nick couldn't let them do that. As immaturely as Lucy had behaved by tattling to her stepmother about him, Nick wasn't going to respond like a child himself by letting his parents defend him. This was something he had to handle directly. "Please don't do that, *Mamm* and *Daed*."

"Why not?" his mother protested. "I shouldn't have to hold my tongue when someone is spreading an unfounded rumor like that about my *suh*! I actually wish I would have trusted my intuition and said as much when I first heard it."

"If Nick doesn't want us to say anything, we shouldn't say anything," his father intervened. "He's a man now and I trust his judgment. Let's go to bed, dear."

Nick's mother furrowed her brow, but instead of arguing she stood, walked over to Nick and planted a kiss on his forehead before saying good-night. Nick shot his father a look of gratitude as he led Nick's mother from the room. After disappointing his parents so often during his *rumspringa*, Nick should have been more pleased to hear his father say he trusted Nick's judgment. But all Nick could think was, *Some* gut *judgment*

I have—I trusted Lucy more than I've ever trusted any woman, and look what happened.

The more he seethed, the more impatient he became to tell Lucy exactly what he thought of her vengeful, juvenile behavior. The thought ate at him until he finally decided it wasn't too late to pay her a visit. He crept out of the house and made it to Lucy's as swiftly as Penny could carry him. It was after nine o'clock, but a light shone in the window, and a few moments after Nick knocked, Lucy opened the door.

She'd barely stepped outside before he hurled his accusation at her. "It's one thing if you're so inherently suspicious you'd make up stories about me and an *Englischer*, but it's another thing to be so vindictive that you'd tell my parents I was courting Jenny Nelson. I thought you were different, I really did."

Lucy's arms were folded like a shield across her chest. "What are you going on about?"

"Don't give me that wide-eyed innocent look. You're not fooling me. You told Betty I was dating Jenny Nelson—you *thought* I was dating Jenny Nelson—knowing full well she'd run right over and blab about it to my *mamm*. If you wanted to ruin my *Grischtdaag*, you failed. You might not know me very well, but my parents do and they don't believe a word you said."

"I didn't tell *anyone* about you and Jenny Nelson, but I wish I had," Lucy exclaimed. "I wish someone would finally expose how irresponsible, immature and self-centered you are. You haven't changed a bit since you were Naughty Nick Burkholder. It wasn't cute when you were a *kind* and it isn't cute now."

"Talk about not changing! You're the same uptight,

self-righteous tattletale you've always been!" Nick jeered. "Keep it up, Lucy, and a pretend courtship is all you'll ever have!"

Nick turned and jumped down the stairs two at a time. He worked Penny into such a hard run that when they came to a quick stop before turning onto a side road, the box containing the teacup he'd gotten Lucy slid out from beneath the seat. He stomped on it, repeatedly and hard, as if he were putting out a fire.

Then, his anger temporarily extinguished, Nick guided Penny wearily the rest of the way home.

Chapter Eleven

Lucy had no desire to get out of bed on Friday morning. The party at the soup kitchen—which Nick had completely ruined for her—was over. She'd delivered her donation to the organizer of the festival auction on Thursday morning. And her fake courtship with Nick had ended. Not even the thought of Bridget coming was enough to motivate Lucy to leave her cozy nest of quilts. Depleted of holiday gladness, Lucy wished she could skip Christmas altogether this year. Or she at least wished she could mark the occasion with individual prayer and Bible study instead of celebrating with anyone else, even her family members.

"What's wrong?" Katura asked, brushing her hair as she sat on the edge of Lucy's bed. "You're usually the first one up. I actually made breakfast this morning."

Despite Katura's recent change of attitude, Lucy didn't quite know if she could trust her enough to confide in her. But tears spilled down her cheeks, leaving her little choice.

"Nick and I..." she blubbered, unable to continue. She'd been preparing to say they'd broken up ever since they began their phony courtship, but now that it had happened for real, she couldn't speak the words. "It's over."

"Oh, Lucy," Katura clucked empathetically. "Are you sure? Maybe it's just a disagreement. Maybe it will pass."

"*Neh*, there's no getting past this," Lucy said, sniffing. Then, putting on a facade of resilience, she added, "I'm okay. You should go now. You're going to be late for work."

Katura secured her *kapp* with a pin and stood up. "Why don't you *kumme* caroling with us tonight? *Grischtdaag* music always makes you happy, and there's a big party afterward at one of the *Englischers'* apartments."

"*Neh*, that wouldn't be fair. I didn't attend any of the rehearsals. I didn't participate in them, anyway."

"That's okay, you have such a pretty voice you don't need practice. You love caroling. Please *kumme*."

Lucy sighed, aware her stepsister hadn't changed her crafty ways overnight. Katura preferred to ride with Frederick, but she knew Betty wouldn't let Mildred go out on her own. Lucy couldn't blame Katura for wanting to spend time alone with her suitor, so, in the spirit of Christmas, she figured she could summon enough goodwill to help Katura enjoy an evening out with Frederick. What's more, Lucy was suddenly filled with a stubborn resolve not to allow her "breakup" with Nick to ruin any more of her pre-*Grischtdaag* festivities. "Okay, I'll go," she agreed.

But when Mildred told Betty their plans for the evening, Betty objected. "I don't like the idea of you going to a party at an *Englischer*'s home, Mildred. And Lucy probably wants to go out with Nick tonight, don't you, Lucy?"

"Nick's...working late tonight," Lucy guessed, glad Katura wasn't in the room to mention their breakup. "I really don't mind accompanying Mildred."

"Maybe not, but you're still as pale as can be. It doesn't seem wise for you to be traipsing around outdoors in this weather."

Seeing the disappointment in Mildred's eyes, Lucy countered, "The fresh air will put a little color in my cheeks."

"Please, *Mamm*," pleaded Mildred. "If we promise to be home by midnight, can we go?"

"Eleven o'clock," Betty compromised. She set down the dishcloth and pointed her finger at the girls. "Not a moment later. And I want the two of you to stick together, do you hear me?"

"Jah, Mamm," Mildred promised. To Lucy she said, "This is going to be a blast! *Denki* for going with me, Lucy."

But as they journeyed to the central meeting place, the parking lot behind the mercantile, Lucy regretted her decision. For one thing, Betty was right about the bitterly cold weather. For another, the first person she saw when she arrived was Dan, who gave her an enthusiastic wave, causing her to feel even worse. Nick had been partly right; she'd put on a big act, falling into Dan's arms on Wednesday night at the soup kitchen. It wasn't because she liked Dan; it was because she hoped her theatrics would make *Nick* realize other young men cared about her, too. She doubted Dan thought twice about it, but seeing him brought unpleasant associations of Nick to mind.

"Hi, Lucy. It's *gut* to have you join us," Dan said. He was standing on the periphery of the large group of singers milling about the parking lot. "Would you like to share my song sheets? I've marked which stanzas we'll be singing since I can't remember and I don't want to embarrass myself."

"Denki," she replied. Since this was the final night of caroling, the youth were visiting homes in the Amish section of Willow Creek before journeying over to the more industrialized side of town, where they'd sing to shoppers entering and leaving a small strip mall.

Shuffling her feet to circulate blood to her toes, Lucy scanned the crowd and inhaled sharply when she spotted a young hatless redhead. But when she realized it was an *Englischer*, she let her breath out again. Relieved Nick was nowhere in sight, Lucy relaxed enough to concentrate on the words of the carols, which announced the joy of Christ's birth. Her Christmas might not be turning out the way she had hoped it would, but she had the promise of God's love to sustain her. *Romance might be fleeting, but the love of the Lord endures forever*, she reminded herself.

Still, as the large group moved from house to house and then journeyed to the mall, Lucy kept thinking about the sweet, vulnerable look on Nick's face when he'd confided how much he disliked his singing voice. She'd gotten to know a side of him other people didn't know—or at least, they never mentioned—and a knot of nostalgia twisted deep within her heart. She was glad when the group ended its final carol.

The large three-story duplex where the party was held afterward was crowded with *Englisch* and Amish carolers, as well as dozens of other *Englisch* young people Lucy assumed were home from college for the holiday. Music blasted in every room, and the *Englischers* had pushed the furniture against the walls so they had space to dance in the living room. Others lounged on the stairway or gathered near the fireplace holding drinks Lucy assumed from the smell were alcoholic. As crammed in as they were, everyone was jubilant and friendly.

In fact, they were *too* friendly for Lucy's comfort; one of the *Englischers* tugged Mildred's hand and told her he had room next to him on the sofa if she didn't mind squeezing in real close. When her stepsister merely giggled in reply, Lucy understood why Betty had been so hesitant to allow her youngest daughter to attend this party. *Nick might think it's okay to be involved with an* Englischer, *but Betty's counting on me to keep Mildred from making a mistake like that*, she thought. She resigned herself to spending an hour sticking to Mildred like glue, but after that, they were both going home.

Since Kevin knew Nick had completed the cabin repairs and because he had nowhere else to go anyway, Nick remained at the hardware store long after their father left for the day. He even told Kevin he'd handle the shop on his own, but to his surprise, Kevin declined the offer.

"After all you've done for me, the least I can do is help out here on one of the busiest nights of the year," Kevin insisted. The brothers agreed to keep the store open extra late in order to accommodate the scores of panicked *Englisch* shoppers who needed to purchase last-minute hardware essentials for Christmas, including tree light bulb replacements, batteries for their children's toys and additional gifts for the men in their families.

As they were finally closing up, Kevin announced he was going to the after-caroling gathering on West Elm Street. Nick knew the place; an *Englisch* college student and his roommate lived there and they frequently hosted big, raucous parties. "You should *kumme*. You'll have a lot of *schpass* now that you don't have to pretend you're courting Lucy anymore. I've heard that *meed* from as far away as Shady Valley are going to be there."

"*Neh*. You go on by yourself." Nick said, advising, "Just don't get into any trouble."

"I won't. I've learned my lesson," Kevin promised. He seemed to hedge before asking, "Are you okay? You seem a little down."

"I'm just beat," Nick glumly replied.

On the way home he allowed Penny to trot at a fast clip, but the velocity didn't bring Nick the sense of excitement it usually did. Instead, he recalled how much Lucy enjoyed it when Penny galloped at top speed. *Dan might have a great singing voice, but Lucy isn't going to have nearly as much fun riding in his courting buggy as she did in mine.* Just thinking about Dan and Lucy embittered Nick and he suddenly decided, *Kevin's right. I should go to the party. It'll be a lot more* schpass *without having to hang around pious, priggish Lucy Knepp.*

He turned the buggy around and headed in the direction of West Elm Street. Brian's house was so crowded Nick could barely squeeze through the door, but when he did, the first Amish person he crossed paths with was Melinda Schrock.

"Hi, Nick. I didn't recognize you without Lucy at your side. She's clear across the room." She took a sip of soda through a straw before adding, "But you better be careful, because your other girlfriend is here, too."

Nick fell right into her trap. "My *other* girlfriend?" he asked.

"*Jah.* Jenny Nelson," Melinda tittered. "Neither of them has probably seen you yet. There's still time to escape. I won't say a word, I promise."

Nick's mouth dropped open. He hadn't expected Lucy's false rumor to travel quite that fast, and he wondered if her stepsisters were responsible. "Who told you Jenny Nelson is my girlfriend?"

"I figured it out myself," Melinda bragged. "It was so obvious—although your *mamm* sure seemed surprised. I hope I didn't get you in any trouble." Melinda's voice dripped with complacence, not contrition.

As she turned to elbow her way back through the sea of people, Nick tried to collect his thoughts. He was so stunned to discover it was Melinda, not Lucy, who had started the rumor about him and Jenny that he might have collapsed to his knees if it weren't for the crush of people pressing in on all sides, forcing him to remain upright. It hit him like a lightning bolt: he'd wrongly accused Lucy just as she'd wrongly accused him. But his accusation was worse, because it was completely unfounded, whereas Nick had been at least partly to blame for Lucy suspecting he was interested in Jenny. After all, Nick wouldn't confirm he'd been completely honest with Lucy when she'd asked him to. And Lucy *had* seen Jenny hugging him the day he returned her key. Other than the fact Betty Knepp wanted to talk to

Nick's mother, what reason did he have to assume Lucy had started a rumor about him and Jenny?

I have to get to her, he thought. *Even if she doesn't believe me about Jenny, I owe Lucy an apology.* Excusing himself as he knocked into people, Nick picked his way through the crowd. *Lucy's so tiny, I'll never see her*, he thought, raising himself on his toes to peer over the shoulders of the group of *Englischers* in front of him.

It took nearly fifteen minutes, but he finally located her chatting with Mildred, Eve and Dan. After greeting them he said, "Lucy, may I speak with you a moment?" He had no idea how or where he'd find a private place to talk, but the other three graciously turned their backs and began edging away.

"I have nothing to say to you," Lucy replied. She tried to walk away, but the room was so thick with people she didn't get very far.

"Could you at least listen to me?" Nick implored, trailing behind. The music was so loud he had to shout to be heard.

"Stop following me!" Lucy tried to continue weaving through the crowd, but a cluster of brawny *Englischers* wearing sweatshirts emblazoned with the name of a local college on the back stood shoulder to shoulder, forming an impenetrable wall in front of the door leading to the hall. Realizing there was no way around them, Lucy turned back and faced Nick, who encircled her wrists with his hands.

"Luce, please hear me out," he begged. Just then someone behind him wrapped her fingers around his bicep.

"Hey, Nick. Am I glad to see you!" It was Jenny Nelson.

Before he could stop Lucy, she tore from his grasp and ducked beneath the arms of one of the students as he lifted a drink to his mouth, tunneling past the young men.

"Hi, Jenny. Look, I, um, I've got to go—" he said, but it was too late. He'd lost sight of Lucy in the swell of partygoers.

Jenny laughed. "You can't go anywhere fast in this place. But I won't keep you long. I just wanted to tell you how great the cabin looks. My mother didn't have a clue anything ever happened, especially because we were dragging in so many boxes of decorations it was hard to tell if anything was amiss or not."

"I'm glad it all worked out," Nick said. *If only everything had worked out that well for me.*

After they wished each other a merry Christmas, Nick searched in vain for Lucy. Moving at a snail's pace from room to room without finding her, he finally decided he'd wait outside. She'd have to come out eventually. But it was Mildred, not Lucy, who emerged an hour later to unhitch their horse.

When Nick asked where Lucy was, Mildred said, "I assumed she'd left ages ago—with you. Now I'm going to have to go back in there and try to find her." She shivered. "Some of those guys give me the creeps. The way they bump into you when you're trying to get past them, it's like they're doing it on purpose."

Nick knew exactly what she meant and she was probably right. "You go on," he said, motioning toward the Knepps' buggy. "I'll go get Lucy and bring her home."

Mildred brightened. "*Denki*, Nick. I'd really appreciate that."

The fact Mildred didn't argue proved she knew nothing about Nick and Lucy's breakup; otherwise, she would have waited for her stepsister instead of letting Nick take Lucy home. Feeling even guiltier that he had suspected Lucy of telling anyone about him and Jenny, Nick urgently jostled his way through the crowd, desperate to apologize.

What Lucy lacked in height or strength she made up for in fury, doggedly prodding her way past bony elbows, avoiding sloshed drinks and sidestepping embracing couples as she dug her way from room to room in search of Mildred, but her stepsister was nowhere to be found. Lucy knew the rule of thumb for being lost was to stay in one place, but she didn't want Nick to catch up to her. Especially not with Jenny Nelson in tow.

How can he keep denying what I can see with my own eyes? Maybe that was just it; maybe when he approached Lucy, Nick was going to come clean about his relationship with Jenny. Lucy didn't want to hear it. Not yet. She didn't want him to apologize because she wasn't ready to forgive him. Not for being dishonest about his relationship with Jenny and not for accusing Lucy of telling anyone about it.

So she kept searching for Mildred as best she could, growing increasingly frustrated. The house was thrumming with the pulse of what the *Englisch* considered music and on the basement level people were smoking, which caused Lucy to cough uncontrollably. Someone handed her a mug of something—peppermint schnapps, they called it—but after one vile sniff, she realized it was alcoholic and set it down without drinking it, coughing even harder. Finally, she cut a path to the balcony. She anticipated no one would be outside since it was so cold, but there were so many people huddled on the little rectangle of wood Lucy feared it would collapse, spilling them onto the concrete two stories below. But she couldn't reenter the smoky house until her lungs cleared.

Lucy peered down at the driveway. *Is that Dan leaving?* she wondered, since it was difficult to tell from above whose buggy was whose. She had to find Mildred and get out of there, but when she turned, she noticed an *Englisch* couple was kissing passionately right in front of the door, blocking anyone from leaving. Everyone else was engaged in chatter and didn't seem to give them any heed. Too modest to interrupt the couple's embrace, Lucy stayed where she was, wiggling her toes and hugging her cloak to her chest to warm herself. By the time the couple finally moved, Lucy felt as if her bones were icicles.

Poking her way through the room, she prayed in vain to find Mildred. Lucy stood in the threshold of the door leading to one of the bedrooms, which was surprisingly empty except for a lone man who appeared to be asleep next to a pile of coats on the bed. Lucy shivered and turned to find herself face-to-face—or actually face-to-chest—with an *Englischer*.

"Are you lost?" he asked, slurring his words.

"*Neh*, I was just looking for someone."

"Well, you found him," the young man said, extending his arms.

"Excuse me." Lucy tried to dodge around him.

The young man didn't budge. "You're awfully cute, but you should ditch these." Before Lucy could stop him, he reached down and removed her glasses. "There, just like I thought. You have beautiful eyes."

The room was a blur. "I'd like those back." Lucy tried to sound firm, but she heard the quaver in her own voice.

"How about a trade? You give me a kiss, I'll give you your glasses," the *Englischer* said. Lucy didn't know whether he was teasing or not, and her stomach churned with a sickening feeling.

"Please give them to me, now," she repeated in what she hoped was a demanding tone.

"Please give me a kiss, now," the *Englischer* said, mimicking her tone. Then he pointed upward. "We're under the mistletoe, see? You have to kiss me."

"No, she doesn't," a male declared adamantly. Lucy couldn't see him clearly but she recognized the voice. It was Nick. Just when she didn't think this evening could get any worse, *he* had to turn up again. *If he thinks I'm going to feel indebted toward him for* kumming *to my rescue, he couldn't be more deluded.*

"Sorry, it was just a joke," the *Englischer* said, handing Lucy her glasses. She put them on immediately and propelled herself past both of them.

"Wait," Nick called loud enough for her to hear above the music's hammering beat. "You can't leave—"

"That's what you think," Lucy retorted. She jabbed her way through the crowd to the kitchen door, and then ran down the steps and along the path leading to the driveway. She was so frazzled she must have forgotten where she'd hitched her horse because she didn't see it anywhere.

"Lucy!" Nick called again, a couple paces behind her. "Mildred took the buggy. I told her I'd bring you home."

She spun to face him and shouted, "You had no right to do that! Now leave me alone." She stormed across the lawn and scurried along the sidewalk, leaving Nick behind. She'd trekked several blocks when a horse came clopping along from behind and then flew by her. It was Penny and Nick. But instead of continuing down the main stretch of pavement, they stopped about an eighth of a mile up the road and Lucy realized Nick was climbing down and coming her way. She'd have to pass him in order to continue her journey home.

"Be reasonable, Lucy," he said. "You can't walk all the way home."

"Don't you dare tell me what I can do," she shouted. She was so fed up with everyone deciding what she was or wasn't capable of doing. She'd show him! When she passed his buggy without getting in, Nick climbed in and followed her as she made her way down the street. *Penny must hate walking so slowly.* But that was Nick's fault, not hers. She thought, *He can follow me all the way home if he wants, but he's* narrish *if he thinks I'm going to break down and accept a ride from him.*

She must have walked for over an hour before the cold air made it so difficult to breathe she struggled to take in enough air. A tear dribbled down her cheek and then another and another before her eyes released a flood. Defeated, she wiped her face with her sleeve before marching toward the buggy and boarding the carriage. "If you say so much as one word to me, I'm going to jump out," she warned in a raspy voice.

Nick honored her demand although two or three

times when her coughing became especially ragged, she felt him studying her. She turned her face and angled her body so he couldn't see she was fighting not to cry.

"You can let me off here," she said, indicating the end of her lane, but Nick brought the buggy up to the turnaround by the back porch. They hadn't even come to a full stop when Betty darted outside, a cloak covering her nightclothes.

"Where in the world have you been?" she demanded to know. "You were supposed to make sure Mildred got home safely!"

Lucy was annoyed. Mildred and Katura had gotten away with missing their curfew on countless occasions, but the one and only time it appeared Lucy didn't follow instructions, her stepmother worked herself into a tizzy. It wasn't fair.

"Mildred *did* get home safely, didn't she?" Lucy asked sarcastically.

Betty balked. "Young lady, you wouldn't be assuming that tone if your *daed* were still awake. I'd hate to think how worried he'd be. I told you to be home by eleven and it's after midnight!"

Lucy resented being scolded in front of Nick. Mildred was the one who had left without Lucy, not the other way around. *Why should I get all the blame, just because I'm older and more responsible?* But she did realize Mildred wasn't to blame for Lucy missing their curfew; if Lucy hadn't been so adamant about not accepting a ride from Nick, she probably would have arrived home a few minutes after Mildred did.

"It wasn't Lucy's fault," he piped up. "It was mine.

I told Mildred go to ahead home. I'm the reason Lucy was so late. I'm very sorry."

First Nick had played the role of her hero in front of the boorish *Englischer* and now he was being chivalrous in front of Betty. If Lucy hadn't known how deceiving Nick's appearance could be, she might have been grateful to him. But nothing he did now could change Lucy's perception of what kind of man he was. Besides, technically he was right: he *had* told Mildred to go home, which ultimately caused Lucy to miss her curfew.

Betty apparently wasn't taken in by his apology, either. "You *will* be sorry if it ever happens again!"

"It won't," Lucy said emphatically before she followed Betty inside and quietly shut the door behind them.

Betty apparently wasn't done with her tirade. "I should have known it was a bad idea for Nick to court you. He's completely unreliable. I expected this kind of behavior from him, but I thought you'd have a *gut* influence on him. I never imagined he'd influence *you*."

Lucy felt a stitch of culpability, knowing she would have been home earlier if she had accepted his ride the first time. "It wasn't entirely his fault," she said weakly.

"There's no need to defend him, Lucy," Betty said. "I won't tell your *daed* about this, but I expect you to exercise better judgment in the future. You're not so desperate to keep a suitor that you'd abandon your common sense. This incident almost makes me sorry I invited the Burkholders over for dessert after the festival tomorrow night!"

"You did?" Lucy gulped. She had no idea.

"*Jah*. I wanted to surprise you. You've been such a

gut sport about attending all of the social events for my side of the family over the years I thought it was time we had some of *your* friends over. Nick's mother agreed it was a lovely idea. Her sons have to close the shop first, but they'll join us here after we return from Piney Hill."

"It *is* a lovely idea. *Denki*, Betty," Lucy said, her eyes brimming with tears. As touched as she was by Betty's gesture, she couldn't fathom how she'd explain to her stepmother why Nick wouldn't actually show up. But maybe she wouldn't have to; maybe he'd be a gentleman and make an excuse for his absence. After all, excuses were his specialty.

Too tired to worry about the situation now, Lucy said good-night and slogged upstairs, but despite her exhaustion it took a long time for her to drift off. Her lack of sleep combined with her apprehension about the Burkholders' visit put Lucy in a foul mood the next day. The festival should have been cause for celebration, not dread, but Lucy wished the event were already over. Since Frederick had picked up Katura, Mildred and Lucy had plenty of room to themselves in the back seat of the buggy. On the way to Piney Hill, Lucy's father, Betty and Mildred sang a medley of carols while Lucy bit her tongue and tried not to cry. She could hardly taste the Philly cheesesteak sandwiches they bought from one of the vendors as they strolled the festival grounds. Even when the auctioneer announced the highest bid for her tablecloth-and-napkin set was $1200, Lucy felt the knot tightening in her stomach.

They were heading back to their buggy when their paths intersected with Dan and Eve's. Was Lucy imagining things or did they just quickly drop hands? When

Eve gave her a wink, confirming what she thought she saw, Lucy smiled in spite of herself. She couldn't envision a better couple, even if Eve had to return to Ohio soon. *Maybe long-distance relationships are the best kind*, she thought wryly.

"Lucy, it's great your contribution raised so much money!" Dan exclaimed heartily.

"Denki," Lucy said, and wished them both a merry Christmas. She was quiet the rest of the way back to the buggy, wondering how she was going to tell everyone she and Nick were no longer courting. She knew she should get it over with now, to spare everyone the awkwardness when the rest of the Burkholders arrived without Nick.

"Daed, Betty, there's something I need to tell you," she began, but she was interrupted by a shout across the field.

"Lucy!" She glimpsed a flash of red hair. Nick?

But no, it was Kevin. "I'm glad I found you. Nick wants to give you a ride home," he said, pointing toward a parking lot on the opposite side of the grounds.

Lucy hesitated. The last thing she wanted was to talk to Nick, but maybe he'd worked out an excuse for the evening. She'd do anything not to have to admit their breakup in front of their entire families tonight.

"You go ahead and ride with Nick," Betty insisted. With levity in her tone indicating all was forgiven, she added, "Just don't *kumme* home too late."

"I won't," Lucy promised, following Kevin.

When they were out of earshot of the others, he stopped and said, "Listen, Lucy, I know you probably don't want to see Nick, but you've got him all wrong—"

Lucy butted in, fuming, "Whatever Nick has told you, you don't know half of the story."

"He hasn't told me anything, but I have eyes. I have ears. And unfortunately, some of our peers have big mouths. So I know enough to tell you you've got him all wrong."

Lucy began to contradict him again, but Kevin spoke over her, saying, "He isn't interested in Jenny Nelson and he never was. He wasn't using you to see her and he wasn't fixing her cabin because of some affection he holds for her. He was fixing it because I started a fire in it and he didn't want our parents to find out because my *daed*'s been under a lot of stress. Nick didn't want me to get into trouble, so he couldn't tell anyone about it, not even you."

Lucy had the sensation the earth was shifting beneath her feet. "Oh, *neh*," was all she could say again and again as Kevin's words sunk in. No, Nick hadn't been entirely honest with Lucy about the cause of the cabin fire, but that was because he was trying to help Kevin, not hurt her. He was protecting his brother, just as he'd tried to protect Lucy the night before when he told Betty it was his fault she was out so late. Lucy had called him immature and self-centered, but she was the one who had behaved like a spoiled brat.

"Where did he park his buggy?" she asked Kevin.

"Uh, about that…" Kevin faltered. "When I said he wanted to give you a ride home, I was making a guess. I mean, I think he will want to give you a ride, but—"

"Just tell me where he is," Lucy interrupted.

"He's still at the store," Kevin admitted. "If we leave now, we can make it there before he closes up and leaves."

"Let's run!" Lucy called, and she took off so quickly toward the parking lot Kevin could hardly keep up with her.

Nick was removing Penny's blanket when Kevin's buggy turned into the special hitching lot for horses behind the mercantile. Nick had grown increasingly nauseated ever since that morning when his mother told him she'd accepted a family invitation to the Knepps' house. *So* that *was why Betty Knepp wanted to talk to* Mamm *on Thursday,* he realized. All day he'd brooded about how he was going to avoid attending the gathering, but as it turned out, his stomachache gave him a legitimate excuse. He'd insisted his brother leave the store early, so he was surprised to see Kevin's buggy returning.

But it was Lucy, not Kevin, who got down and came toward him. As much as Nick had wanted to speak to Lucy at the party the evening before, he wanted to avoid speaking to her tonight. His stomach was in knots, he heart was wrung out and he felt like he was on the brink of either crying or throwing up. Quickly he adjusted Penny's harness straps and climbed into the carriage.

"Nick, can I talk to you?" Lucy implored, standing at the side of the buggy.

"Not now. I don't feel good and I was just leaving," he replied, looking straight ahead.

"Please don't," she said, but he picked up the reins. Lucy was suddenly in front of the buggy holding her palms toward him. "Stop," she commanded Penny.

"Lucy, get out of the way," Nick shouted. "You're going to get hurt."

"I don't care," she shouted back. "I'd rather get hurt physically than to let you to feel hurt emotionally from all of the things I said. The accusations I made. Please, Nick. Please let me talk to you."

Nick reset the parking brake and jumped down. Penny was agitated, so he stroked her neck, avoiding Lucy's eyes. "I'm listening," he said.

"Kevin told me you weren't interested in Jenny. He told me he started the fire, too. But he shouldn't have had to. I should have known—I *did* know, deep down—I was wrong about you. I called you immature and irresponsible and self-centered, but those words describe me, not you. You were right, I have such a self-righteous attitude. But I'm no better than anyone—in fact, I'm worse." Lucy was gasping, her words tumbling over each other.

"Slow down," he said, dropping Penny's rein and moving closer to Lucy's side. "You need to catch your breath."

She was really gasping now so he put his hand on her shoulder, the way he'd calm his horse. "Whoa," he said. "Breathe in and out, Luce. In and out."

When her breathing steadied, she said, "I'm so sorry for saying such *baremlich* things to you. I was just so incredulous that you would have genuinely liked me that I jumped to conclusions to prove that it was all a sham. It wasn't because I doubted you. It was because I doubted... I doubted anything so *gut* could be true."

Nick searched her face, which was contorted into a grimace. "I can see why you'd think I was interested in Jenny. I wasn't totally honest with you from the beginning. I'm so sorry about that and I'm so sorry about accusing you of helping spread false rumors about Jenny and me. I know now you didn't do that. But, just like you said, I should have known all along. That's not the kind of person you are. You're…you're not like any woman I know."

Lucy half coughed, half sobbed. "*Jah*, I'm sickly and dull."

"What?" Nick nearly hollered in bewilderment. "I didn't mean that at all. You may have health challenges, but I haven't seen them stop you from doing whatever you want to do. In fact, you work harder than most *meed* I know. And you're the most interesting woman I've ever met. I mean, you're quiet sometimes, but I like how thoughtful you are. You can also be really surprising, so being with you is an adventure. But more than anything, I feel like I can completely be myself when I'm with you." Then he emphasized, "I feel like I can be *better* than myself when I'm with you."

"There's no need for you to be better than yourself. You're *wunderbaar* just as you are," Lucy immediately responded, gazing earnestly at him. "You're so popular and outgoing sometimes I can't believe you're having as much *schpass* with me as I'm having whenever I'm with you. But you're not *just* fun to be around. You're also caring and hardworking and dedicated to the people you love."

Lucy lowered her eyes shyly, and Nick's chest swelled as he allowed her words to settle over him. She paused before lamenting, "I would do anything to take back the awful things I said this past week."

"So would I. But since we can't, how about if we start completely anew right now, this minute?" Nick asked. "Complete honesty?"

Lucy nodded. "I can say with complete honesty that

even though our relationship began as a fake courtship, it's become the most real thing I've ever experienced."

"I can say that it's the most real thing I've ever experienced, too. The only thing fake about it was that it was fake."

Lucy giggled and rubbed her arms. "I'm getting cold. Will you take me home?"

"I'd be happy to, after I do this." Nick bent down and kissed her. Then he straightened and said, "In the interest of being completely honest, I have to confess I just lied. I don't want to take you home. I want to keep kissing you."

"I appreciate your honesty," Lucy said. She stood on tiptoe and wrapped her arms around his neck, and they kissed several more times. Funny, but Nick's stomach-ache had vanished completely.

Lucy never knew a Christmas like this one. When she returned home, she was surprised to find Bridget had arrived a day early—she wasn't expected until late Sunday afternoon—and Lucy threw her arms around her cousin before tugging her into the hall.

"Listen, I was going to tell you this in private, but you're going to find out shortly anyway. Nick Burk-holder is courting me. He's not like he used to be. I mean, not like when he was courting you and started walking out with Naomi Renno before you'd even broken up."

Bridget scrunched her forehead a moment before her eyes lit up. "Oh, *jah*, I remember that now. I'd forgotten all about it."

"You forgot Nick was seeing someone else behind your back? But you were devastated!" Lucy didn't want to bring up unhappy memories, but she couldn't be-lieve Bridget was being so blasé about it.

Bridget waved her hand. "I'm sure I felt crushed at the time, but hearts mend. He wasn't the right one for me. Besides, I found out a long time ago he wasn't really walking out with Naomi. It was just a rumor, a complete falsehood, and I jumped to conclusions. That wasn't fair. I'm glad you're not as judgmental as I was."

"Oh, I'm not so sure about that!" Lucy said, laugh-ing.

After Nick's parents departed and Lucy's went to bed, the young people continued playing board games until almost midnight. When it was time for Nick to leave, Lucy zipped upstairs and returned with some-thing in her hand. They stepped onto the porch while the others said their goodbyes.

"Did you notice Kevin and Mildred seem to be en-joying each other's company?" Lucy asked.

"*Jah.* We'll have to keep an eye on them if they wind up courting."

"To be *gut* examples?"

Nick chuckled. "*Neh*, to be sure they don't make the same mistakes we did." He wrapped his arms around Lucy as they observed the stars. They stood in silence and then Lucy gave him the flat little packet she was holding. "It's a sort of *Grischtdaag* gift I made a while ago."

"Aw," Nick moaned, recalling how he'd destroyed the gift he'd bought for her. "Yours will be a little late."

"Your forgiveness is the best gift I could receive. Besides, this is a silly little thing. *Kumme* into the light so you can see it."

Nick moved to the part of the porch where light streamed from the window and he carefully unwrapped the package. It was a handkerchief, and embroidered in the corner was a coppery, galloping horse, his mane flying back, his hooves lifted in speed.

"I know it's a strange gift, but I thought you could use it since you didn't have one to offer me that night I was crying."

"Denki," he murmured. "But I hope nothing makes you tearful when you're with me anymore."

She grinned up at him. "Only the wind against my face," she said. Smiling, Nick bent to kiss her, but she pulled back. "Not in the light—someone will see us."

"Gut," Nick replied. "I hope they do."

Carrie Lighte

Epilogue

In the spring both Nick and Kevin were baptized along with several other Willow Creek young people, and afterward their church hosted a traditional potluck dinner.

"I'm proud you made the choice to commit to following Christ and the Amish church," Nick's mother said to him.

"There was never a question of if I'd commit. It was only a question of when," he replied. "I should have done it long ago, but I'm glad I did it today."

"So am I," his *daed* said.

"Me, too," Lucy added as Nick's parents left to tell Kevin they were grateful he was baptized, too.

"Now that I'm officially considered an adult in the eyes of the church, you know what this means, right?"

"*Jah*. It means you can't let Penny gallop so fast," Lucy joked. "It's not responsible."

"Hardly!" Nick uttered. "My running around days may have *kumme* to an end, but Penny's running doesn't have to. *Neh*, I was going to say now that I'm baptized, there's nothing to keep me from marrying an Amish *maedel*."

Lucy blushed, teasing, "Well, I can think of one thing. You have to find a *maedel* worth marrying, first."

"I already have," Nick said. He didn't kiss her, since that would have been inappropriate for the occasion, but he did lean over and whisper, "I love you, Lucy."

"I love you, too, Nick." She surreptitiously squeezed his arm and gazed into his eyes. It was the first time they'd spoken those words aloud, but it was no rumor they were true.

* * * * *

Don't miss the start of a new Amish miniseries from Carrie Lighte, set in Maine!
The first book is available December 2019 wherever Love Inspired books and ebooks are sold.

Dear Reader,

When I was around Lucy's age, I was sometimes drawn to gregarious, charming men like Nick, who in many ways were a contrast to my reserved, introverted personality. Then I went through a phase where I deliberately avoided that type of man at all costs. Like Lucy and Nick, I eventually realized I couldn't judge a book by its cover one way or the other; I had to get to know the person—and vice versa—on more than a superficial level before determining whether or not to develop a relationship.

Similarly, I'm reminded of Isaiah 53:2, which indicates there was no comeliness about Christ that we would be drawn to Him. Whether that refers to His physical appearance, lineage, societal status or something else, I'm not certain. But I do know He wasn't anything like people expected. Discovering who He is and how much He loves me is the most rewarding joy of my life, as I hope it is for you, too.

Blessings,
Carrie Lighte

COMING NEXT MONTH FROM
Love Inspired®

Available October 15, 2019

THE CHRISTMAS COURTSHIP
by Emma Miller
Caught up in a scandal in her Amish community, Phoebe Miller moves to her cousin's farm in Delaware hoping for forgiveness and a fresh start. The last thing Phoebe expects is to fall for bachelor Joshua Miller. But can their love survive her secret?

HER AMISH CHRISTMAS CHOICE
Colorado Amish Courtships • by Leigh Bale
Inheriting a shop from her grandfather could solve all of Julia Rose's problems—if Martin Hostetler will renovate it. As an *Englischer*, romance with the Amish man is almost impossible, especially with her mother against it. But Martin and his faith are slowly starting to feel like home...

WESTERN CHRISTMAS WISHES
by Brenda Minton and Jill Kemerer
Homecomings bring love for two cowboys in these holiday novellas, where a woman gets more than she bargained for with a foster teen to care for and a handsome cowboy next door, and a bachelor finds an instant family with a single mom and her little girl.

THE TEXAN'S SURPRISE RETURN
Cowboys of Diamondback Ranch • by Jolene Navarro
Returning home with amnesia years after he was declared dead, Xavier De La Rosa is prepared to reconnect with family—but he's stunned to learn he has a wife and triplets. Can he recover his memory in time to reunite his family for Christmas?

HIS CHRISTMAS REDEMPTION
Three Sisters Ranch • by Danica Favorite
Injured at Christmastime, Erin Drummond must rely on her ex-husband's help caring for her nephews. But as they stay on the ranch together, can Erin and Lance find a way to put their tragic past behind them and reclaim their love?

HOMETOWN CHRISTMAS GIFT
Bent Creek Blessings • by Kat Brookes
The last person widow Lainie Dawson thought to ask for help with her troubled child is her brother's friend Jackson Wade—the man she once loved. But when her son bonds with Jackson and begins to heal, Lainie must confront her past— and future—with the man she never forgot.

LICNM1019

Get 4 FREE REWARDS!

We'll send you 2 FREE Books plus 2 FREE Mystery Gifts.

Love Inspired® books feature contemporary inspirational romances with Christian characters facing the challenges of life and love.

FREE
Value Over
$20

SPECIAL EXCERPT FROM

Surprise fatherhood, Southern charm and a heartwarming family Christmas—read on for a sneak peek at Low Country Christmas, *the conclusion to Lee Tobin McClain's Safe Haven series!*

Cash remembered coming out to Ma Dixie's place at Christmas time growing up. The contrast with his own foster family's home had been extreme. There, six themed Christmas trees were spread throughout the house, decorated perfectly by the commercial operation that brought them out each year and took them away after the holidays. That same company had wrapped garlands around the staircase and strung lights outside the house.

It had all been grand. He remembered being shocked and impressed his first year with the family, because it had been so different from the humble holidays back in Alabama. But he hadn't been allowed to invite his brothers over; too much noise and mess, his foster mother had always said. If he wanted to see them, he had to find a ride out to Ma Dixie's, which he had done frequently.

Here, Christmas really felt like Christmas.

He opened another box of ornaments, pulled out an angel made of hard plastic and handed it to Holly to place on the tree.

"Is this your tree topper, Ma?" Holly asked, holding it up.

"Yes, it is. I usually have Pudge put it up, but…could you do it, Cash, honey?"

He did, easily reaching the top of the small tree. "Is Pudge okay?" he asked Ma. "Is that why the place isn't decorated yet? He's too sick to help?"

Ma arranged the last figures in the Nativity scene and sank down onto the couch. "That's part of it. Mostly, it's me feeling blue. I'm not used to Christmas with no kids around."

Holly tilted her head to one side. "Did you have a lot of kids?"

"Dozens," Ma said with a wide smile. "That's the beauty of being a foster parent."

"Oh," Holly said as she sank down onto an ottoman beside Ma. "Do you…not foster anymore?"

Ma sighed. "I really can't with Pudge having all these doctor appointments. I guess maybe we're getting too old for it." She looked wistfully at the tree. "I just, you know, always enjoyed having the little ones around."

Holly looked thoughtful. "Is that why you wanted to take care of Penny? Not to help me out, but to have a little one around?"

"That's part of it," Ma said, "but don't you worry about it. I understand being picky where your child is concerned."

"It's not pickiness," Holly said. "If I were being picky, who better than an experienced foster parent like you?" She reached out and rubbed Ma's arm back and forth, two or three times, an affectionate gesture that made Ma smile.

Cash came over and sat at Holly's side, leaning against the ottoman. His heart, like that of the Grinch in the movie playing muted on the television, seemed to be expanding.

He'd taken plenty of women to high-end Christmas parties and fancy restaurants. But sitting here in Ma Dixie's house, talking with her about holidays and kids and family problems, decorating the tree with her, felt different. Like coming home.

Like coming home, with Holly beside him.

He put that feeling together with the questions his brother and Pudge had been asking. He was getting the horrifying notion that he might be falling in love with Holly. But he wasn't the falling-in-love type, or the settling-down type. And Holly wasn't the type for a short, superficial fling.

So what exactly was he going to do with all these feelings?

Don't miss Lee Tobin McClain's
Low Country Christmas,
available October 2019 from HQN Books!

Looking for inspiration in tales
of hope, faith and heartfelt romance?

Check out **Love Inspired**® and
Love Inspired® **Suspense** books!

New books available every month!

CONNECT WITH US AT:

Facebook.com/groups/HarlequinConnection

 Facebook.com/HarlequinBooks

 Twitter.com/HarlequinBooks

 Instagram.com/HarlequinBooks

Pinterest.com/HarlequinBooks

ReaderService.com

LIGENRE2018R2